Bitter Sweet Vengeance

Cursed Witch Book 1

Tia Silverthorne Bach

BitterSweet Vengeance

Cursed Witch Book 1

Tia Silverthorne Bach

BitterSweet Vengeance
Cursed Witch Book 1
by Tia Silverthorne Bach

Copyright 2018 © Tia Silverthorne Bach
Published February, 2018
ISBN 10: 1985391864
ISBN 13: 978-1985391864

License Notes

This book is licensed for your personal enjoyment only. It may not be copied or re-distributed in any way. Author holds all copyright.

This book is a work of fiction. Names, characters, places, and incidents either are products of the author's imagination or are used fictitiously.

Cover design, editing, and formatting for print and digital by Jo Michaels of INDIE Books Gone Wild
Published by Tia Silverthorne Bach

The unauthorized reproduction or distribution of a copyrighted work is illegal. Criminal copyright infringement, including infringement without monetary gain, is investigated by the FBI and is punishable by fines and federal imprisonment.

Contents

Chapter 1 1

Chapter 2 15

Chapter 3 28

Chapter 4 39

Chapter 5 51

Chapter 6 64

Chapter 7 78

Chapter 8 87

Chapter 9 98

Chapter 10 107

Chapter 11 117

O, vengeance!

Why, what an ass am I! This is most brave,

That I, the son of a dear father murder'd,

Prompted to my revenge by heaven and hell,

Must, like a whore, unpack my heart with words,

And fall a-cursing.

Hamlet (2.2), William Shakespeare

Chapter 1

Vengeance

"I demand revenge!"

I attempted to stay focused through the young woman's tale of woe and mistreatment, yet another harrowing story about despair and terrible wrongs. Not too long prior, I'd perch on the edge of my seat, soaking in every last breath of the damned, from those desperate to strike out against the evil that had stolen a piece of their soul. My skin would tingle with anticipation, my heart skipping a beat, as I conjured up inventive ways to exact justice. Righting wrongs became my obsession.

From my own horrific experience came the power to enact justice, to provide the victim some comeuppance. Once a target myself, I'd sworn to fight against the tyranny of abusers.

As the petite blonde spewed out her story—another tale of an insensitive and uncaring man leaving a young woman stripped of her confidence and self-worth—I listened with little more than numbness. I'd heard it all over the years, but my conscience and doubt had crept in, and I'd decided to investigate the claims, no longer motivated solely by emotionally wrought sob stories. I'd seen the underbelly of being judge, jury, and executioner.

Everything changed the day I discovered the details of my own story, how all had not been as it seemed, how *I* had been the pawn in another's evil game. But truly, it had all started with Dominick, the young boy who stole my heart. His piercing green eyes still haunted my dreams, and my mind lost itself in the memories, the images as vivid as the first time. I slipped back into the past, and it wrapped around me like an old blanket.

※

MY FACE HURT FROM the huge smile that spread as Dominick waved his hands over the tall grasses, commanding them to lie down and create a small patch of a flat area. A soft breeze rustled the remaining stalks as Dominick unfurled the picnic blanket, laying the basket filled with goodies on one corner before taking my hand and pulling me down next to him on the red-and-black checkered material.

"My sweet Natalia." He crooked his finger, summoning me to join him.

My breathing slowed, and I licked my lips, lost in the twinkle in his eyes and his sexy grin.

When I regained the capacity to move my limbs, I placed a knee on either side of his legs and lowered myself to straddle him, wrapping my arms around his neck and pressing my body to his. Energy pulsed around us as I leaned in for a long kiss. It started slow, his soft lips tender and warm, but then the kiss deepened into something hungrier, his tongue playing with mine. Warmed by the sun and physical touch, we delighted in each other for several titillating minutes. Heat spread through my body, leaving me so sensitive to his touch that my skin prickled. A shiver ran down my back as his fingers explored the tender skin on my breasts through the sheer fabric of my dress. Burning from deep within hinted at magic beyond our feelings.

"We have to slow down," he said, his words breathy and rushed in between kisses. "I have plans."

I pulled back and looked into the eyes that had become the window into my own soul, trying to calm my breathing.

"I love you."

Leaning my forehead into his, I whispered the same words back to him, harnessing all my energy to push away. I crawled over to the opposite end of the blanket and started rummaging through the picnic basket, suddenly hungry.

"I love the view," he teased, and I tossed a bag of chips at his head.

We shared a laugh and then devoured our food. Everything about that afternoon was perfect.

As I skipped home later that day, my body light and my heart full, I knew I wanted to give myself wholly to him. I fought to suppress the happiness emanating from me, hoping to avoid another lecture from my mother. She never missed an opportunity to warn me about unrealistic romantic notions. My father had abandoned us in the middle of the night, leaving my mother and me to fend for ourselves. His only parting gift was a massive, leather-bound spell book passed down for generations in his family. When I was little, he'd bring it out and spin tales about my heritage.

As my powers blossomed, they served as a constant reminder to my human mother of the magical scoundrel who contributed to a portion of my DNA. To make things worse, Dominick came from a very powerful family. Or, so he'd warned me early on. I had yet to meet his mysterious parents.

My magic hummed when I was with Dominick, my first indication of the power coursing through my blood. A tingling sensation spread through me as I imagined what might happen when we finally made love. My dreams—both at night and during the day—were filled with the fantasies of how our special night would play out, and even my mom trying to warn me against overly romanticizing the first time in my head never dulled the fantasy.

The next evening, I'd just kissed my mom goodnight when a soft voice beckoned me to the front door. There, just inside, as if someone had slipped the article under the door that second, an envelope appeared. I picked it up, and Dominick's musty smell assaulted my senses. With barely concealed excitement, I rushed up to my bedroom, closed the door, and ripped into the letter.

Inside, words of love flowed on the handwritten note, concluding with a request to meet in the woods near my house. We'd spent most of our days, especially since it was summer, out in nature. Amongst the trees, grasses, and other living things, our bond seemed unbreakable. So, even at that late hour, I didn't give a second thought to rushing into the night to meet my love. After spritzing on a bit of perfume and checking my reflection in the bathroom mirror, I whispered a few chants to ease my mom into a peaceful sleep—thankful, yet again, for my family's spell book. Then, I opened my bedroom window enough to wedge my body through and climbed down the trellis on the side of our house. With a flick of my wrist, I brought the window back down and then leapt to the ground.

As I made my way to the rendezvous point, I chuckled. I could've skipped the romantic notion of shimmying down the trellis and simply walked out the front door, knowing my mother wouldn't wake until morning. But I wanted every detail of that night to be perfect, a memory I'd never want to forget.

With each step, my mind painted a more vivid picture of the evening before me. Everything from the words he'd say to the feel of his skin against mine. A small twinkle of light floated into my vision, bringing me out of my fantasies and back to the path in front of me, and I instinctively knew to follow it. In the distance, I could see more lights, and as I came closer, the brilliant glow intensified. A path with rose petals strewn across the flattened grass came into view. Walking slower to savor every moment and detail, I memorized every nuance of the flickering light of the candles and finally Dominick, his hand stretched out to me.

Barely able to contain myself, I quickened my pace and closed the distance between us. When I got close enough to reach for his hand, he pulled it back.

A foreboding feeling sent shivers down my spine, and a dark shadow descended upon me. I scrambled backward as the shape morphed into a large man, his features blurred and nondescript. He twisted his hand into my hair and yanked, sending shooting pains along the back of my head and down my neck. Frantic, I pleaded with Dominick for help, only to be met with a blank, empty stare. He stood, unmoving, as the man dragged me away, the shadowed forest closing in around me. Darkness stole away the physical details, leaving my mind to conjure up my own images.

As a scream bubbled up inside me and I dropped my jaw to let the terror free, the man stuffed a wad of material into my mouth and tied a fabric piece around my face, covering my eyes and mouth. Pressure weighed on my chest, making it difficult to breathe, and my heart raced. I fought him with everything I had and managed to free myself. I scrambled away, disoriented and nauseated. I clawed at the fabric on my face but failed to loosen it. After only a few frantic, confused steps, the man slammed into me, turning me to face him as he backhanded me. I could taste the salty blood that trickled into my mouth as rough hands forced me to my hands and knees and ripped off my dress and undergarments, the sound of tearing fabric searing into my brain.

Tears slid down my face as my cheek slammed into the ground. My arms gave way, unable to hold myself up any longer. As my privates throbbed with pain, another, larger, something penetrated me. In my heart, I knew it was the attacker's penis, but I forced my mind to other places, to anything other than the violation of my body. My father's spell book became my focus. *Can I remember any spell that might help?* But words and pages blurred as my body screamed out in pain, my mind unable to overtake what was happening to me. Then, I conjured an image of Dominick, of the boy on the picnic blanket.

Why is he allowing this to happen?

My heart shattered as hands dug into my hips, his nasty grunts causing shock waves of nausea to run through me. Then a rising anger. Anger that anyone would think they had the right to something that wasn't theirs.

First fear, and then some unknown force, kept me from using magic. When I tried, emptiness overwhelmed me, like nothing I'd ever known, as if something were blocking me.

Everything stilled, and I dared to think my nightmare might come to an end. A brief sense of relief softened my pain, but then I heard a deep voice say, "Next," and the horror began again. Over and over the brutality continued until my mind grasped onto its best survival technique, and I lost consciousness.

*****

I awoke the next morning to discover myself naked in the middle of the forest. Trying to stand, I fell to my knees, pain coursing through my battered and bruised body. Inhaling a few times, I summoned all my strength and finally made it to my feet, surveying the area around me. Out of the corner of my eye, I saw my sundress, and with wobbly steps, I walked over to pick it up, wrapping the material around me. Like a thunderclap too close by, the sound of fabric ripping boomed in my head, and I pressed my palms against my ears to try and squelch the painful noise. Flashes of the night before played in my brain, and I squeezed my eyes shut, willing the images to stop.

Home seemed so far away, and through sheer determination, I made it there, sneaking in the back door and hurrying up the stairs. As I clicked my door shut, I noticed the clock beside my bed. Seven in the morning. I exhaled, grateful the sleeping spell I conjured would give me a few more hours before I had to face my mother.

I opened my closet door to examine myself in the full-length mirror hanging on the back and dropped the blanket. As it pooled at my feet on the ground, I stood motionless, except for the slight movement of my chest drawing in air. Bruises and puffiness marked my face, and just above my upper lip was a cut with dried blood. Dirt and more dried blood marked my inner thighs and lower legs.

Tears slipped down my face, and although my brain told my legs to move toward the shower, it seemed to take longer than normal for my body to respond. Finally, I stepped onto the cold tile of the bathroom, the iciness of the floor an odd comfort, and cranked the nozzle in the shower as hot as it would go. Steam billowed out, creating a thick cloud, and I stepped in, relishing the scalding sensation against my skin, hoping the hot liquid would burn away any remnants of my attackers. I scrubbed my body until it burned raw, desperate to rid myself of the feeling I knew would never go away.

My mind yearned to make some sense of the evening, of why Dominick would've stood there and let it happen. As the water cooled, a scorching rage built inside me. I turned off the tap, pushed the shower curtain to the side, and stepped out, grabbing a nearby towel. Dripping water from one end of my room to the other, I dug into the back of my closet and pulled out the spell book.

I searched for a truth spell, something I never thought I'd need to use on Dominick. And then I performed a quick locator spell using one of his t-shirts—one I refused to wash and slept in most nights. I had to have answers. With calculated speed, I dressed, grabbed the keys from the hook by the garage door, and then raced to a local coffee shop, the spot the locator spell indicated he'd be.

When I pulled up, I saw his car. I focused on my breathing for several minutes before I gathered the courage to face the boy who'd stolen my heart and then destroyed it. Stepping inside the small café, I spotted him with a group of buddies at a corner table. When he saw me, he stood, and his usual smile graced his face.

I forced down the bile rising in my throat and chanted the words to the truth spell under my breath.

"Natalia, what are you doing here?" He leaned in for a kiss, but I pulled away, clenching my fists to avoid thrusting one into his midsection. *How dare he act so normal after watching me get gang-raped?*

Seeing all his friends watching, and terrified one of them had joined in the night before, I needed a private moment. "Can we talk outside?"

"Sure, hon." He turned to his friends. "Be right back."

"Don't make it quick just for us," Rodney said and high-fived Billy.

My stomach clenched and vomit threatened. With each step, I feared I might buckle under the agony coursing through my body. Finally outside, I drew in a deep breath of fresh air and spun to face Dominick.

"Why didn't you help me last night?" Words I intended to scream barely came out as a whisper.

"Help you with what? I thought we had a great time yesterday."

Fury blinded me, and I slapped him with every ounce of strength I possessed. No longer able to stomach being near him, I turned to run. I heard his pleas for me to return and talk, but I raced to my car, desperate to get away from him. I never wanted to hear his voice again. Tears filled my vision, and I struggled to get my keys out of my pocket, my hands shaking.

A hand touched my shoulder, and I jerked away, spinning around to find Dominick. He bent to pick up the keys and held them out. "Please, Natalia. I don't understand."

I snatched the keys. Determined to create as much space as possible between us, I pressed my butt against the car for leverage and slammed my palms into his chest. Anger surged through my arms, and I could feel my power intensify. In a flash, I threw him twenty feet through the air.

My mouth dropped open, but I quickly recovered, jumping in my car. As I peeled out of the parking lot, I saw his friends rushing out of the café to help him. I slammed my hand on the steering wheel. "Damn him!" I screamed. Not bothering to pull into the driveway, I drove the car half onto the grass just outside my home. Racing inside, I pushed past my mom, who was stumbling around the kitchen, clearly trying to shake off her deep sleep, a coffee mug in hand.

One purpose fueled me, and I tore into my father's book, my legacy, searching for a spell that would make Dominick suffer like I'd suffered. My father's one gift would bring me the peace I needed to move on.

Chapter 2

"Are you even listening to me?"

Her annoying voice yanked me back from my unintended trip into the past. As much as I'd wanted to roll my eyes and dismiss the annoying twit before me, I played my part. "I apologize. What is it exactly that you want me to do?"

"I want you to skewer his ass."

I might have chuckled at the sheer lunacy of the request, but her shrill voice grated my last nerve. As much as I dreaded continuing the conversation, and wondered why I would even try, I'd sleep better knowing I gave her a chance. "So, what did this guy do, may I ask?"

"He slept with my sister!"

Those five words used to be enough to send me over the edge, to have me pulsing with the thrill of carrying out revenge against another thoughtless man. But for every person I helped, I condemned another. Deciding who deserved punishment had become too great a burden to bear, leaving me—and everyone who interacted with me—to suffer the consequences.

Fingers snapped in front of my face, and in reaction, I swatted her hand away.

"I was told you would take my money"—she threw a wad of bills at me—"and make that bastard pay."

"On one who takes revenge, revenge must be taken, or the balance tilts, and chaos ensues." I quoted the missive from memory.

"I command you to take revenge on Connor." She stomped her foot like a toddler demanding their way.

With her declaration, I could feel the tension around my heart, as if clamps were being fastened around it—the same sensation I felt every time. Thanks to my curse, I couldn't deny the woman her desire. And my warning about balance hadn't swayed her.

"As you wish," I said. I wouldn't torture myself with that one. Maybe, just maybe, Connor was the bastard she claimed and deserved the horrific death she'd require. "Should I determine his fate, or do you wish to do so?"

A gleam in her eye, followed by the slight upturn of her lip, made me physically ill. Like a genie trapped in a bottle, I had no choice, unless given it. Whatever wicked deed she requested, I'd have to fulfill. Vengeance simply meant a punishment inflicted or retribution exacted for an injury or wrong, at least according to Webster. I knew every intricacy of the word, of the deed. If left to me, I could decide the punishment. But if commanded, my curse left no room for clarification or due diligence. I must carry out the revenge as specified.

"I want him to rot in Hell."

My body spasmed in reaction, and I couldn't control the constriction of muscles, particularly on my face, in anticipation of the deed. I'd condemned several souls to Hell, and each time, I lost a piece of *my* soul, watching as the person was dragged below by the darkest of demons to an eternity of torment. I played God, although not of my free will, and I wondered if some day He would come to put an end to it.

"Good God. You're pathetic. I was told of your power, and all I see is a woman on the edge of some kind of personal crisis."

If only I could wield my awesome power in other ways, but it came with rules and restrictions.

"Your will shall be done."

"And what proof will I have that our business is complete?"

How dare she?

My fingers twitched to teach her a lesson, but as my mind considered the options, a piercing pain exploded behind my eyes—an excruciating reminder of the boundaries of my power. Refusing to give the twit in front of me one moment of satisfaction, I steeled my gaze on her and dug my fingernails into my palms to counteract the agony.

"My word."

"Not good enough."

I stood, clenching my fists by my side and glowering at her. My power twitched through my body and crackled with blue lights pulsing between my fingertips, like electricity come to life. She took a step back, not knowing what I knew—I couldn't turn the power on her.

After her small retreat, she bumped into a table behind her, and several trinkets fell to the ground. She glanced at them and then straightened her spine and declared, trembling lip and all, "I want to be present, to see it for myself."

Driven by her pain and blinded by her rage, whether justified or not, she had no clue what her request would mean. Had I sensed even a moment of hesitation in her insistence on condemning a man to Hell, or the slightest hint of kindness in her, I would've insisted she sit out the torture. But something about her narrowed eyes, her jutted-out chin, and her lips pressed together in a hateful smirk rendered me silent. I knew all too well that some couldn't realize the horror of vengeance, what it does to those who sought it, without gruesome detail.

"As you wish. I'll—"

"Actually, *I* will lure them into Pritchett Woods. There, you'll send them both to Hell as I watch. Once it's done, I'll give you the rest of your fee," she said as she gathered her things.

"Them?" I asked, although I knew the answer.

"Connor and my sister." With a flip of her head, her hair swirled out behind her, almost hitting me in the face. She marched out of the room as I settled back into my chair.

As much as I wanted to condemn the young woman's hatred, I couldn't deny how much the emotion had filled me at times. How I'd let it consume me. Memories of Dominick's last breaths hit me hard, knocking the wind out of me. My eyes rolled into the back of my head as time yanked me backward.

<hr />

AN OPEN SPELL BOOK. *A detailed path to seek revenge. I procure the necessary supplies and summon the witch. She appears before me briefly.*

"What you seek, you shall find in the northeastern copse of trees in your beloved forest."

I run downstairs, only to have my mom block the doorway and demand to know where I'm going. I shove her out of the way and race outside, clutching my spell book and supplies. With each step, the forest grows darker, and I come upon a gathering of trees I've never noticed before. Trunks and leaves bent and curved around each other, creating a tapestry of greenery. As I step closer, I see an opening and a light. I bend down and push aside growth. As I do, the gap seems to get wider and eventually leads into a domed room of wood. A loud slam echoes behind me. I twist to see the opening has closed, and I appear to be in an encased tomb with no way out. My pulse speeds up, and my heart nearly stops when I hear a voice.

"What is it your desire of me, my child?"

I spin my body to face her, a beautiful woman with black hair, porcelain skin, and eyes the color of wheat kissed by the sun. She motions for me to sit in the chair next to her.

"Revenge."

"Ah, my specialty. You do understand such a request comes with a price."

Flashes of Dominick's face right before I was taken and brutalized swirled in my mind, cementing my determination. "Whatever it is, I'll pay."

She reached out, took my hands, and immediately let go, her eyes wide, and her mouth forming an O shape. "Much power courses through you, my dear. Who sent you here?"

"My father," *I say as I hold the spell book before her.*

She motions for me to hand it to her, and when I do, she trails her finger over the cover as her lips curl into a smile.

"So, you're the one I've waited for."

I open my mouth to ask what she meant, but she speaks before I can form a single word.

"Your destiny has led you here, a destiny foretold to me. Great power will be bestowed upon you *in addition to ending the lives of those who harmed you. Every single one of them."*

"How do you know who they are? That there are more than one?" Many more questions bounce around in my head, but one in particular rises to the forefront. Saying it out loud causes pain to surge through my body. "Do you know what they did to me?"

"You'll understand soon enough. You must tell me their names."

My hands tremble, and I put them under my thighs to try and stop the motion. "I only know one name, one face. The rest I never saw."

"Once you have this power, you can seek out the others. Bring the boy to me, to this same place, tomorrow night, and I'll take care of it."

"And the cost?"

"You shall take my place."

<hr />

A RUSH OF WIND AND banging brought me back to the present, my hands curled into the fabric of my dress.

"Your dinner, Miss Natalia."

Rebecca carried in a tray holding a silver dome, a French roll, a glass of lemonade, and a bowl of strawberries. As she set it down on the side table to my left, she took the silver lid off, revealing my favorite chili.

"Thank you, my dear."

"Are you okay? You seemed… caught up in your thoughts when I walked in. I hope the last visitor didn't upset you."

I forced a smile, hoping to ease the girl's worries. She'd come to me a couple of years before, seeking her own revenge, an act she let me talk her out of. Then, a year later, she came back to me, declaring she was forever in my debt. She'd sought revenge against her mother, blaming her for not stopping Rebecca's abuse at the hand of her stepfather. I'd asked her to take a night to reconsider, and she'd done so.

Her mother had pulled a gun on the girl's stepfather that night, promising that if he ever touched one of them again, he'd get his brains blown out. It had only taken two weeks until Rebecca's mother carried out the threat.

"Please, don't worry about me. And how is your mother, my dear?"

Rebecca began to tidy up the room, her happiness like a burst of energy. "She's so excited to marry Fred, and you know I think he's amazing.

The wedding is in a few months. Please, won't you come?"

I'd cut myself off from society a long time before then, and Rebecca was my only bright light. Still, I couldn't bear the torture of happiness, something denied to me long ago.

"You know I can't."

"Well, I'll bring you some cake and goodies then. My mom wanted me to thank you for your very generous gift."

It was the least I could do for Rebecca's family. Little did she know that I had also purchased them a home and arranged for an attorney in town to inform them of it just before the wedding.

"Sounds good."

"Are you sure you're okay? That lady who just left gave me the creeps."

"I've handled worse than her."

She kneeled in front of me, taking my hands. "There's nothing I won't do for you. You always tell me you have no choice in this revenge business, but I know, deep down, your heart isn't in it. Please, stop before nothing of you is left."

Such a wise girl. *No matter what happens to me, I'll always know I saved at least one soul*, I thought.

"Not much is, but I'm grateful for the joy you bring me. Now rush along. I know there must be so much to be done for the wedding."

Her hesitation sent a tingle of joy into my heart.

"Get, you silly girl," I said.

"I'll be back tomorrow with some breakfast. Leave me a list of anything else you need, and I'll do some shopping this week, too. See you later." She waved as she skipped out of the kitchen.

In her, I could see the young girl I used to be. All the potential for a great life. Everything one night had ripped away from me.

I ate my dinner and then went into my study, sauntering over to my bookcase and running my fingers along the spines of my collection. I lived through the pages of the books, my only connection with the outside world. Rebecca purchased them for me, and she knew I had one hard-and-fast rule: the story must have a happily ever after.

My perusal stopped on a classic, one I hadn't read in a while. *The Wizard of Oz*. I pulled it off the shelf and took it into my bedroom. After indulging in a long, hot shower, I slipped into my most comfortable robe and snuggled under the covers, opening the book.

Dorothy lived in the midst…

About fifty pages in, my eyelids began to flutter, and I drifted off to sleep.

~~~

"Mom, just give Dominick this note."

"Natalia, please, tell me what's going on."

As if my heart had turned to stone, I ignore her pleas, thrusting the letter asking Dominick to meet me in the forest into her hands.

"Please. I need you to do this for me."

She nods in a very slow motion, and I slip out the door.

Within minutes, I arrive at the designated area, much faster than should've been possible. The witch is already there.

"You understand that once the deed is done, you'll take my power and my place."

"Yes, I do."

Dominick's voice filters through the night, calling out my name.

"I'm over here," the witch says, using my voice.

He steps into the clearing. "Mother, what are you doing here?"

Before I can react, the witch lifts her hand, which in turn lifts him off the ground. "What—"

He doesn't utter another sound; as she snaps her fingers, his neck cracks, his head hanging at an awkward angle. She then relaxes her hand, and he drops to the ground.

"Your son?" My voice trembles, and numbness settles over my body. I can't move, as if my feet are rooted to the ground in concrete. "Dominick is your son?"

"It was the only way to lift my curse. You'll understand someday."

A woman with bright red hair and dark brown eyes suddenly appears before me. She puts one hand on Dominick's mother's chest and another on mine. Intense pain ricochets through my body, and I fall to the ground, curling into a ball. My head lolls to the side, and all I can see is Dominick's body lying in front of me.

Chapter 3

My eyes sprang open, and I tried to calm my breathing. With each reoccurrence of the nightmare that plagued many of my nights, I reacted differently. At first, I'd awoken with a smile. No matter how odd the circumstances, I knew Dominick deserved what happened to him. His death had been quick, his pain over in an instant. Nothing like what I'd endured at the hands of his friends.

That nightmare had spurred me to commit countless acts of revenge for years afterward as I tried to quench an unending thirst for justice. But with each passing day since that fateful night, my reaction began to morph—agony was replaced with questions.

Discovering the truth about Dominick became my obsession, and the lack of answers only served to further cripple my spirit and my will to live. I stood in the shadows the day his friends mourned his loss. So many people from the community had showed up to pay their respects, to watch his coffin lowered into the hard ground. No parents, but teachers, students, and even my mother.

After Dominick's death, I awoke to an intense humming of power, my body charged with whatever the witch had done. I'd stuck around for the funeral, wanting the feeling of satisfaction, but I only grew angry as people mourned him, having no clue what he'd done. Each tear that rolled down my mother's cheek only served to stoke my fury. My mother *and* father had forsaken me. I bolted, determined to leave the town behind and revel in my newfound power. But as I ran into the forest, a gust encapsulated me, and my vision went dark. A burning sensation swept over me, and each bone in my body cracked, as if splintering. I lost consciousness.

When I awoke, I was in my house, my prison, and every time I attempted to leave, a force slammed me back inside. The only exception: when I needed to go somewhere to carry out another's revenge plot.

I stood, my limbs shaking as I walked to the window. Sunshine and beautiful colors—leaves in fall shades, the blue sky, a red robin perched on a branch—greeted me. Yet another curse. If I opened my door, a wall of darkness met me. But anytime, day or night, my window showed me nothing but beauty.

Memories pounded through my aching head. No matter how much I tried to stop them or push them away, they gained momentum, playing with increasing speed through my mind on an endless loop of fast forward.

Demons tearing a man limb from limb as his screams echoed through the forest. Then the eerie snapping of the monsters reattaching body parts and starting the process all over again.

Gazing upon an angelic face, the most handsome man I'd ever seen, and then me pulling the trigger, the bullet smashing into his features and forever maiming him. Knowing his beauty would never lure in another gave me intense satisfaction.

Whether they deserved it or not—a judgment I no longer trusted myself to discern, nor wanted to make—didn't lessen the images of the punishments I inflicted.

Forcing a husband to watch as his wife drove a flame-red piece of metal up into herself, scorching any future chance of passion or children. A revenge requested by her husband upon finding out their daughter had been sired by her lover.

A reenactment of Joan of Arc's burning at the stake, a request by a college student overly enamored with history and the best way to strike out against her fellow student, a girl who had bulled half the school. Flames had engulfed her as light danced in her accuser's eyes.

All those horrific images assaulted me until I collapsed, landing with a loud thud as my knees hit the hardwood floor beneath me. Whether any of my victims had deserved their punishment of not, carrying out the acts against them chipped away at my resolve. *Have I not become the very thing I'd sought to punish?* I lowered my head to rest on the wood and pressed my fingers against my temples, trying to send a pulse through to erase the torture, to end the pain.

As always, when I drew upon my power for anything other than its intended purpose, nothing happened outside of the pain intended to remind me of my restrictions. My sight blinded with atrocities, I reached for something, anything, to help me stand, and my hand settled on what felt like a piece of banister on the stair railing. I attempted to pull myself up, but reality and the past blurred until my brain could no longer differentiate between the two. What at first appeared to be a banister became a long sword, which I thrust through the heart of a young girl as her boyfriend watched with unabashed glee—his smile so bright it hurt to look.

"Oh my God." I heard a voice screech.

Rebecca? I felt hands touching me, sweeping my hair back from my face.

"Natalia, I'm here. What can I do? What's wrong?"

Her facial features sharpened, and I could almost make out her face.

"My carving knife. You must get it for me," I yelled as I pushed her away.

"Knife, but—"

"Now!"

Death, destruction, devastation… It all pelted me like a downpour of rain. Each drop chipping away at what was left of my soul.

"I have it, but…" Rebecca said.

"Give it to me." I reached forward, still unable to clear my vision. A cool piece of steel settled into my palm, and I grasped it, feeling a slight sense of relief when the sharp edge cut into my skin.

Falling back into a seated position, I lifted the knife, clutching the handle with both hands, and thrust it at my chest, eager for it to be over. As it hit, it bounced off, and I lost my grip. Soft clanging sounded as it landed a few feet away.

"No!" The scream ripped from my body, and I clambered to my hands and knees, crawling over to the sound and splaying my fingers on the floor in a desperate search for the weapon. Tears, along with a never-ending source of memories, clouded my vision

I found my weapon and threw my head back, pressing the knife to one end of my throat and pulling it sideways, making a slashing motion against the delicate skin there. But the blade glided across, not even causing me the slightest pinch.

"Stop this!" Rebecca yelled, taking the knife from me.

My head pounded, and I succumbed to the weight, falling to my side and curling into a ball.

"Please, Natalia. Please, let me help you. After everything you've done for—"

"You have no clue what I've done, young lady. No clue." I said each word with the same cadence and tone, like the sound of hitting the same key on a piano in a timed sequence.

Rebecca slid down to my level, wrapping her arms around me from behind. "Then tell me. I want to help."

Although I desired her warm touch, needed it desperately, it singed my skin, as if I didn't deserve even that morsel of joy, of living. I rolled away and sat up, bringing my knees into my chest as items in the room came into focus and my head cleared.

"I'm cursed, and sometimes it's more than I can bear," I said, shocking myself with the burst of honesty.

Rebecca stood and offered me a hand, which I took. She led me to the kitchen table, pulled a chair out for me, and asked me to sit. I struggled to remember the time or day. Once I was seated, she took the kettle from the stovetop and filled it in the sink. I heard the familiar click of the gas surface lighting before she turned back to face me.

"I brought some groceries to cook you breakfast. All the makings for an omelet and some warm bread." She disappeared around the corner and then came back in carrying several plastic bags.

I watched in awe as she switched into service mode.

"Does ham, spinach, and cheddar cheese sound good?"

After trying unsuccessfully to push out a word, I nodded.

She busied herself with breakfast preparation for several minutes before bringing over a slice of bread with butter and the promised omelet. A titillating aroma pervaded my senses, and I reached for the fork with a shaky hand and pierced a small section of eggs, lifting them to my mouth.

"I'm not leaving until you tell me everything. I just watched you try to kill yourself twice. Yet there's not even a scratch on you. Nothing. I saw the knife bounce off you like a ball." She placed a hand on my arm. "Nothing you say will change how I feel about you, my indebtedness to you."

I chewed slowly, laying the fork back down on the table. Never, not in the five years since Dominick's death, had I shared my story with anyone. Then again, nobody had asked or cared.

"It's a long and brutal tale."

"I've got nothing but time and a very open heart," Rebecca said.

"What about your mother's wedding? You must have so much to do."

"Please, you know me. I'm so far ahead in planning I can be here as long as you want me to today."

Want. Something I rarely considered. Maybe Rebecca could offer an insight to my life.

"Years ago, five to be exact, I fell in love with the most handsome young man. His name was Dominick. Everything about our love seemed pure and beautiful. Until…"

The horror of that night settled on me, and I remembered every painful detail. Again. "One night, the night I planned to give myself to him completely, I was attacked and brutally raped by multiple men. Dominick stood there and watched, his expression void of any emotion."

Rebecca's sharp intake of breath made me look away to avoid seeing her pity.

"To this day, I don't understand it. When I tried to confront him about it, he seemed clueless. I've played that scene over and over in my mind, and nothing makes sense."

"Is there nobody you can ask? And you said you were cursed…"

"Spurred by an indescribable pain, I searched my father's spell book and called forth a witch to seek revenge. She promised me such, but then when Dominick showed up, I realized the witch was his mother."

"His mother?" The words came out as a shocked whisper, and Rebecca moved her hand to cover mine. I pulled back, unaccustomed to and uncomfortable with the intimacy.

"She snapped his neck, promised me unfathomable power, and cursed me to forever carry out revenge requests. If someone requests revenge, no matter how horrific or unjustified, I must carry it out."

"What happens when you don't?"

"I have no choice. I must. I'm compelled. For years, I relished the task." As ashamed as I felt, I wanted Rebecca to hear every sordid detail. I didn't deserve her pity or love. "But then I realized not all who sought justice were innocent, and very few cases were clean and simple."

Rebecca and I both jumped when the kettle spewed a blast of steam. I knocked over the small salt shaker to my left, and her hand flew to her chest. She rushed to turn off the heat, took a couple of deep breaths, and set about making tea. Chamomile and lavender scents filled the air, and I inhaled the soothing aroma.

After placing the mugs on the table, Rebecca sat next to me, taking a sip of her steaming tea before asking, "Is that why you wanted to change my mind? To keep me from doing something I'd always regret?"

She'd been the only one I'd ever persuaded to walk away, and I'd endured great physical and mental pain to do so. But ultimately, she'd saved herself by never actually making the request, by taking the time to consider her choice.

"You give me too much credit. Only you could make that decision. And had you asked, I couldn't have stopped it."

"There has to be something you can do. Can't you talk to the witch who cursed you and ask how to be released? There's always some kind of way, some caveat." She smacked her hand on the table, and my mug bounced up a bit. I steadied it as she stood and paced behind me. "I know how much you love the books I collect for you. A lot of times I'll read them ahead, to make sure you get your happily ever after. There's always a way, some kink in the rules. You've paid your price. You deserve more than this. You—"

"I've already asked. And the price to end this curse is simply too great."

Chapter 4

All movement and sound ceased behind me. Out of the corner of my eye, I saw Rebecca lower herself back into her chair. Her shoulders slumped, and she bit on her lower lip. I took a sip of tea, breathing in the calming aroma. As I set the cup back on the table, I could detect Rebecca's brain working overtime to make sense of everything, to figure a way back to her happily ever after beliefs. Her body language spoke volumes as she tapped her foot and grasped her tea mug, running her fingertip along the rim.

"What exactly did the witch say? We can figure this out."

A woman after my own heart; she seemed desperate to find a loophole. I shook my head and pressed my lips together, stopping the momentum of the smile threatening to form.

"Come on," I said, picking up my mug and tilting my head toward the front sitting area. "Maybe the universe will work through you to see something I can't."

A flicker of hope danced into my heart, and I squelched it with images of Selene sitting in the dark red wingback chair I headed toward. I'd never known her name until she answered my summons and announced herself. She looked years younger than when she condemned her son to death and me to a lifetime of heartbreak. Her raven hair cascaded behind her, and the dress she wore accentuated every curve from her ample breasts to her small waist.

"Just a few days ago, Selene—Dominick's mother and the witch who cursed me—sat in that very chair," I said, pointing to the offensive piece of furniture. "I explained to her that I wished to be set free from my curse. That I'd seen the error of my ways."

Rebecca came around to stand in front of me. "And what did she say?"

I tore my eyes away from the chair and the woman who still sat there in my vision. "She laughed. A long, drawn-out cackle, very much reminiscent of the witches in literature." Having just re-read *The Wizard of Oz*, those crones were still in the forefront of my mind, all Selene had lacked was green skin and a bad wardrobe. She had the beauty of Glenda with the laugh and evil nature of the Wicked Witch.

"You're nothing like what I imagined a witch to be," Rebecca said, leading me over to the loveseat and patting the cushion next to her as she sat down.

"I'm nothing like what *I* imagined a witch to be." I thought about the spell book and all the hopes and dreams it represented, especially when combined with Dominick's power. How perfect it felt when our magic intertwined, cocooning us in pure happiness. I shook my head, trying to clear my mind and refocus. "But back to Selene. She asked how I felt about Dominick, about what I had done to him.

"I told her I regretted seeking revenge, but I still wished for answers, to know why he'd allow something so horrible to happen to me. She drummed her fingers on the armrest and snickered, before saying, 'There's a wish I can grant. If it's an answer you seek, an answer you will have.'

"At that point, she placed her index fingers to my temples, and blinding light filled my vision, my head aching with what felt like a migraine. Then, I saw Dominick pacing in the field on the night of my attack. He had a bouquet of roses in his hands and seemed nervous. From out of the shadows, his mother steps up to him. And I can hear their whole conversation. The spell she put on him to watch before she called forth demons—"

My voice cracked. If I possessed the power to damn Selene to Hell for what she'd done to me, to her son, I wouldn't have hesitated. Anger burned deep within me at her treachery, especially because she made me live through it again. Only one thing gave me peace: knowing Dominick didn't participate in, or have any knowledge of, what had happened, because she'd wiped his memory at the end.

"I'm so sorry," Rebecca said, scooting closer to me.

"She made me watch it and experience every moment of it again, except this time, I saw the distorted attackers, the five demons who each took a turn raping me."

"Have you prayed about being released from your curse?" she asked.

Her question caught me off guard. "Prayed?"

"Our God is a good God. He knows you don't deserve this. If anyone does, it's Selene. You're a victim."

I hung my head, shame filling every pore of my body. "I was a victim until the minute I took justice into my own hands and sought revenge. Dominick's death is ultimately on me, and I've paid for it many times over. I'm sure God's heart broke for me when those demons violated me, but I'm also sure it shattered when I took matters into my hands. And yes, I've prayed. For years. I prayed many nights for His assistance and some way out of this curse. But I fear the only escape will be a deal with the Devil, for he seems to have my soul firmly in his grasp."

A lump formed in my throat, and it grew to an unbearable size as I spoke. Swallowing took great effort. Rebecca seemed to sense my discomfort because she excused herself and came back with water.

"Thank you," I said after a sip.

Tears glistened in her eyes.

"Please, don't feel sorry for me. You can see why I deserve my sentence. I'm paying for my own mistake, something I fear I'll do for eternity in the bowels of Hell, but I wish to be released from the agony of inflicting pain on others, whether they deserve it or not.

"But there's more. Selene released me from the vision and then explained that she was promised she could keep her awesome power and curse another if she simply gave up something she loved. Her next words chilled me to the bone. 'I loved power more than Dominick, though I loved him more than any other.'"

Rebecca had been walking around the room as I told my story, and she came to an abrupt stop, spinning to face me. "She killed him without a moment's hesitation?"

"It seems so. I told her I didn't want power, only to be released from the curse. And she did give me a way, but I refused, so it seems I'm doomed to my fate until death beckons me home."

Dropping to her knees before me, Rebecca took my hands. And that time I let her. "What could possibly be worse than what you do?"

I remembered the smirk on Selene's face as she explained my choice. "She said, 'You can only end the curse by taking the life of someone you love.'" I took a deep breath, remembering the words. "I refuse. I couldn't live with myself if I took the life of someone I cared about. I did that once. There's no worse punishment."

I only wish my choice had been that simple. When I announced my conviction to Selene, she laughed again, throwing her head back, her entire body quaking with her amusement.

"Ah, you see, I've decided already. I mean you called me here and asked how you could end your curse. You must kill a loved one," she'd said when she regained some composure. *"There is one who desires your soul. He'll have it, but you can choose when. Power awaits you with him."*

"And if I murder a loved one. What then?"

"You no longer have to carry out revenge. Free will shall be reinstated. Though I make no promises for a happy ending, just one where you have a choice."

I remembered the exchange and the intense gaze that bore into me. My fate was sealed.

Lost in my thoughts, the sound of Rebecca's voice startled me.

"I can help, at least make your situation tolerable. How about I vet the people who seek you out? Tell them I'm your assistant and need to have some questions answered before they can see you. I can do research and make sure their request is justified."

"So, I condemn *you* to be the judge and executioner, to decide who deserves punishment? I won't. I didn't save you to condemn you. It's a burden you do *not* understand, nor do I want you to."

"But I want to help, to pay you back for all you've to done for me."

I slammed my hand on the cushion and stood, pointing to the front door. "Either respect my wishes, or leave and don't come back." I wouldn't be responsible for another's pain. But I hated the shrill sound of my voice and seeing the hurt in Rebecca's eyes. Still, I'd choose loneliness over hurting her any day.

"I'm sorry. I only wanted to help," she said, her voice trembling.

It seemed inflicting pain came naturally to me, whether I intended to or not. "No, I'm the one who's sorry. I knew your heart from the moment you walked through my door. Saving you is the only thing I've done right in many, many years, and I won't taint that by seeking your help. However, I do like your idea." Possibilities swirled in my mind. "Maybe you could do the research and pass it along. I'll determine who comes through to see me. And before you suggest I just turn everyone away, I tried that once. The pain was unbearable… as if my power turned its ugliness on me, a raging cancer burning through my body. Yet I couldn't die."

I thought I'd outmaneuvered the curse when I refused to see anyone. But the pain had become too much, and I acquiesced. The second time I tried it, I withstood the agony longer, but a man came to me seeking revenge at my lowest point. I tried to resist, but my body took over, its need for survival stronger than my own desire to stop the curse.

"So, do we have a deal? You meet with those who seek my power and get their information. We could even do the research together. But the burden of decision will be mine alone. Understand?"

She wiped away the moisture from her eyes and nodded. "It's the least I can do."

Then, she threw open her arms and embraced me. My body jerked in response, so unaccustomed to the sensation. Nobody had touched me with such affection since Dominick. Rebecca pulled away and hopped around a little, like a young child who needed to go the bathroom.

"I'll be back with your dinner tonight, and we can discuss the best way to go about this. I left some stuff for you in the fridge for lunch, but if you need anything, please, let me know." She left, offering a quick wave before shutting the door.

With her came hope, a disastrous emotion for my situation. Every time I'd allowed it to worm its way in, my heart suffered, splintering over and over. Pain never ceased to amaze me. Whenever I thought I could sink no deeper into its web, my suffering intensified, its depths an endless well.

And most days I welcomed the ache, the hardening of my heart and soul. It made my fate easier to accept. I took the stairs slowly, each step a reminder of the limits to my existence—my life encompassed in this structure except for the occasional release to nature to perform unspeakable acts. At the next level, I wandered over to the largest window in the house, a massive picture window that served as a display of the woods surrounding my property. Several branches from the giant oak in front came within ten feet of the house, as if nature extended an arm just beyond my reach.

For several weeks, I'd watched as a red robin visited her nest, protecting her babies. They'd hatched only two days prior, and the mom landed with a juicy worm for their breakfast, their tiny beaks barely peeking up over the carefully constructed home of twigs and leaves. Life. Nature's beauty. I took in a cleansing breath, considering how I might change my fate and utilize Rebecca's help. Maybe I would even pore through the spell book again for something, anything, that might assist us. Although I'd scoured it many times before, to no avail.

A flutter of happiness floated from my heart and through my veins, producing a smile. Sweet chirping only served to intensify the effect as a ray of sunshine filtered through the thick leaves and shined a spotlight on the babies. Without warning, a dark cloud moved into view, blocking the sun. Chirping stopped, and the mother flitted her head about nervously. In the blink of an eye, a large black raven swooped in and used its beak to snap the robin's neck just before doing the same to each of her babies.

I threw a hand to my mouth and gasped as the raven sauntered to the end of the branch, spreading its wings as if to mock me. A harsh caw escaped its beak, and we locked eyes. As if to drive its point home, it went back, grabbed the dead mom's body, pulled it over, and tossed it into the window, slamming it into the glass. I jerked back, the raven flew away, and a thunderstorm moved in, rain pelting the window and causing the bird guts to run down the glass.

Familiar emotions of anger and hatred pulsed through my body, and I spun around, wishing I had somewhere to run, some way to escape. I shook my fist at the heavens. "Why do you mock me? What I wouldn't do to just be outside, to escape these four walls for even a few minutes. Can I not even get the smallest of favors?" The volume behind my words escalated until I was screaming, the veins pulsing in my neck.

As I took in a deep breath, my fists clenched at my sides, the doorbell chimed, causing my heart to jump. Grinding my teeth together, I bounded down the stairs and threw open the door.

Cecily stood there, her hands on her hips. Worst sight for my troubled heart—the annoying blonde hell bent on destruction.

"Let's go. We have a date with Hell."

Chapter 5

LIKE THE RAVEN swooping in, Cecily pushed past me as if she owned the place, holding an envelope above her head.

"I've got something for you. But only *after* I see Connor and Elizabeth pay." Thanks to the venom spewing from her mouth and the crazed look in her bulging eyes, I half-expected her head to begin spinning and a demon to show itself.

"Your husband—"

Cecily bent over, high-pitched giggles erupting from her small body. "That son of a bitch is *not* my husband. He might have been, had he not chosen my sister!"

It was official: Fate mocked me. I asked for a moment in nature, and in came the wrath of the Devil to lead me outside to condemn her boyfriend—not even her husband—to Hell. I could only imagine her sister was the better choice, and Connor deserved more than a demon escort into eternal fire. But even thinking about going against her wishes caused intense pounding in my head. Squinting against the pressure, I excused myself to gather my supplies.

In actuality, I required nothing outside my own power, but I needed a few seconds to breathe. For the second time that day, I climbed the stairs. As I turned the corner to head into my bedroom, deciding to change into more practical clothes, I saw the remaining bird guts crusted on the glass. Damn the Universe, Fate, God… whatever.

Rummaging through my drawers, I finally settled on some yoga pants, a black tank, and a dark hoodie. I pulled my hair back into a low bun and stared at myself in the bathroom mirror. Lines marred my young face, not from age—my power slowed that process—but from stress and the weight of my actions. I leaned closer to my reflection, searching my eyes for a spark, any sign that the former me still resided somewhere. But the brilliant blue had dulled over the years to dark gray.

Stalling will only delay the inevitable, I told myself and stood straighter, exhaling deeply. Nothing would stop what had to be done. Thanks to the cruelty of my curse, even a last-minute retraction from the requestor couldn't stop what had been asked of me.

Three years before—and one of the first cases to break my angry dedication to exacting revenge—a young girl, Phoebe, commanded me to kill her father. She'd left the punishment up to me but requested to be present. After hearing of the man's atrocities—he'd raped his daughter multiple times—I decided to ram a hot poker into him repeatedly and then break his neck. Such was my insatiable need to inflict pain and suffering on perpetrators. After six thrusts of the glowing red metal rod, the man howled in pain—which satisfied something deep inside me, causing a huge smile to spread. Then, Phoebe's mother showed up, pulling a man behind her who was bound and gagged. She yelled for me to stop.

I twisted around to stare at the face of the man I tormented. My gaze flew back and forth for several agonizing seconds before a sinking feeling settled in the pit of my stomach, leaving me swallowing down nausea. Phoebe stood, her mouth hanging open and her eyes wide. Her mother, through tears and struggling to speak, explained that Phoebe's uncle, her father's identical twin, had been the one raping her.

She cried out for me to fix things, to take the one who deserved it. I would've, with pleasure, but nothing could've stopped her father's fate at that point. I ended him quickly and turned my vengeance on his brother, but I'd tossed and turned that night with the first twinges of regret.

Something deep inside had told me the forthcoming events would leave me stripped bare, hope once again destroyed. But without options, I made my way back downstairs to Cecily, who was tapping her foot and pointing to her watch.

"Tick, tock. They should meet us at the rendezvous point just after five, so we have about fifteen minutes to—"

I grabbed her arm to end the insufferable sound of her voice and blinked, transporting us to the meeting place. When I broke contact, she stepped back, twisting her head from side to side and taking in the scenery.

"Wow," she said, breathless. "I was *not* expecting that."

If I could've transferred my curse to her, I would've done it in a heartbeat. Although she might take a lot longer than I did to be burdened by it, I believed she'd ultimately see the error of her ways. And if not, she could answer for it in the very place she'd condemned her boyfriend and sister to languish.

Thanks to the dark cloak of winter, darkness surrounded us, the trees blocking out any moonlight. Soft giggling sounded in the distance.

"Ah, Abigail. I'd know that laugh anywhere," Cecily said, a smirk appearing on her face. "Connor should be arriving soon. I sent them each a note, as if written by the other, to meet here. Serves them right."

A note. *Dominick.* A request to meet, only to be ambushed by death. I pushed away the memories and focused on the task at hand. Or tried to. My heart, as it had more and more, struggled against the inevitable, trying to convince my brain to find an escape. Searing pain muffled my desire to fight against the impending deed, causing me to wish for a speedy end for Connor, Abigail, and myself.

"Abigail." I heard the male voice second before he slipped into the small clearing. "Cecily." He halted at the sight of her and took a step back, his eyes darting around the space and landing on Abigail as she joined us.

His eyes then found me.

I recognized the familiar look of panic as it settled into his features and gestures: his shaking hand motioning for Abigail to come to him, his eyes twitching, and his chest rising up and down more rapidly than before.

"What do you want with us?" he yelled, taking a step toward me.

Cecily stepped between her victims and me. "She's here to give you both what you deserve."

"You know I don't love you. I never have. Your father forced us into an engagement because you told him you were pregnant."

Please, please, don't make me listen, I screamed in my head. Their story would only serve to add to the torment of my prior misdeeds.

"You did love me. Slept with me on multiple occasions as I—"

"I slept with you twice. Alcohol was involved, although that's no excuse. And I immediately ended things. I regret ever touching you!" He spat and hugged Abigail to his back, a shield between her and any possible assailant. "I love Abigail. Always have."

Cecily threw herself at him, clawing and scratching at his face, and Abigail started crying, running up to me. "Please, do something. She's crazy. She already tried to kill him once." Her trembling voice and tears reignited my heart and its desire, and I threw a hand up to knock Cecily down. When I did, my breathing became labored, as if a hand were wrapped around my neck. I fell to my knees, struggling to breathe.

Connor grabbed Abigail and raced out of the clearing. I watched them intently, hoping they'd get away, but they ran into a force—like an invisible wall—and slammed into the ground. He got back up and tried again with the same results.

"Kill them!" Cecily yelled.

My free hand—the one not desperately clawing at my neck—rose of its own accord, the ground shaking beneath us. I struggled against it, against the increasing pain and suffocation, but something else took over. My hand lifted inch by inch, as if yanking a weight buried deep. The scent of sulfur permeated the air. Evil. With everything left in me, I fought, but the smell only intensified.

Take me instead. I tried to scream the words, but they only sounded in my head, my voice too weak and my throat clamoring for oxygen. It was agony to pan my eyes around the area, to watch the torment inflicted upon two people in love.

Connor desperately attacked the unseen barrier to his escape while Abigail huddled near him, her body racked with sobs.

In the center of the clearing, Cecily twirled, holding her dress up and squealing like a little girl dancing in the park. Determined, and begging for the sweet release of death, I crawled toward her, trying to cover the few feet separating us, wanting to strike her down for daring to delight in the scene. I struggled as if swimming in quicksand. As two dark forms began to ascend from the earth, I tried to stand, placing a knee on the ground for support. With each inch I gained, the dark shapes further developed into their true demon forms. Then an unexpected third demon, much bigger than the other two, appeared, locking eyes with me.

Over the years, I'd seen demons materialize in many forms. Everything from a more dog-like creature to a chiseled, handsome man with black wings. Before me stood an older man with rugged features, pock-marked skin, black hair, stubby horns at the top of his head, and hands accentuated with nasty claws.

"Ah, my sweet Natalia." He inhaled deeply, his nostrils flaring. "I long for the day you will join me." He bent closer and ran a razor-sharp claw tip down my cheek, light enough not to break the skin but still leave an impression, before leaning in to run his tongue from my forehead to my neck. "You smell and taste so good."

His words assaulted my gut, reminding me of the night that forever changed my life. Terror clawed at my throat, and I forced it away. Something about him seemed familiar, but I ignored it, wanting nothing more than to allow him the pleasure of ending my life.

"Take me." I choked the words out.

"Oh, I will. Ever since the first time I sampled you, thanks to the lovely Selene, I knew I wanted to taste you for eternity."

Bile rose in my throat, further complicating my ability to breathe, as realization sunk in. My gut fully realizing its initial response to him. He'd been one of the demons who raped me.

"You son of a—" I hoped the words came out and hadn't just sounded in my head; everything blurred as I began to black out.

"Oh, dear, we can't have you leave us." He waved his hand in front of my face. Oxygen rushed into my lungs, and I gasped in response. "You have to finish the task." He moved to the side, clearing my line of vision.

One demon had ripped off Abigail's clothes and pounded into her as she screamed, and the other demon threw Connor's body against a nearby tree, over and over again, the sound of his cracking bones causing a shiver to race up my spine. I moved my hands to cover my ears, but the older demon pinned my arms to my sides.

"Enjoy the fruits of your labors, my child. My minions have been looking forward to this one. Nothing satisfies us more than a good man and an innocent. It's been a long time since a virgin joined us."

I squeezed my eyes shut as a lump formed in my throat. He'd taken my virginity from me, one of the first of many devastating losses at his and Selene's hands. If Abigail was a virgin, too, that meant Cecily had also lied about Connor sleeping with the girl. I felt wretched. But the demon would have no part of me cowering away, and he peeled my eyelids open, forcing me to watch.

"I offer myself in their place. Let them go," I said.

"No!" Cecily's shrill scream drew my eyes to her. "I command you to fulfill your agreement. I command you!" She stomped her foot, again reminding me of a toddler having a fit.

With a wave of his hand, the demon holding me hostage slammed Cecily into the ground, knocking her unconscious. "A favor for you. You're welcome. I couldn't stand another second of her shrill voice." He shivered. "And your offer, though tempting, isn't one I can cash in. As much as I'd like to have you now."

"Some witch curse is stronger than a demon. Must be infuriating," I said, surprising myself with the bold words. A movement ahead caught my eye, and I saw Connor break free, hobbling to Abigail to throw his tattered body over her, only to be tossed to the side, his arm ripped off at the shoulder, muscle and sinew dangling from the stump.

"How pathetic that you can't take me now." I dug deep to keep any hint of desperation out of my voice.

"You're crafty, child, but I'm on to you. Pass the curse as Selene instructed, and you shall be a queen in Hell. As broken as you are, you'll come to embrace it. And you'll possess power like you've never known."

He cupped his clawed hand behind my neck, a couple of his talons piercing my skin, and slammed his lips into mine. The more I struggled, the more force he applied. When he loosened his grip, I pulled back enough to spit in his face.

"I *will* have you again, bitch!" he roared, and in a flash, he was gone.

Scrambling to my feet, I raced toward the demons, my arms raised. "Back to the bowels of Hell," I commanded. The demons gathered their prizes, and I stood helpless as they dragged Connor and Abigail, kicking and screaming, into the earth. As the fissure closed, the area settled into an eerie stillness. Nothing moved for several seconds, as if the air had been ripped away into the void. Not one leaf rustled or branch swayed.

Full of pent-up energy, I turned to face Cecily's prone body. I turned her over, grabbed her shoulders, and shook, wanting her fully awake for what I was about to say. When her eyes fluttered open, I let the bottled-up words explode forth.

"Are you happy?" I yelled, pressing my face close to hers. "You just condemned two good people to Hell. I meant what I said." I took a final step and yanked her hair back. "On one who takes revenge, revenge must be taken. And I hope your reward is many times worse than what you just inflicted on Connor and your sister."

"Let me go, you evil witch." I shoved her away, and she shook her head, pushed her shoulders back, and smoothed her skirt. "As if you can judge me, I'm sure you've done horrible things."

"I have. Things you can't even imagine." I backhanded her, enjoying the shocked look on her face enough to deal with the ensuing pain. "Now, go. And never call upon me again. I want the next time I see you to be in the pits of Hell." I waved my hand, and she was gone.

Back to her miserable life, as I would have to go back to mine.

Chapter 6

I FELT MYSELF FADE, wishing for the sweet release of death, but light burst into my vision as I transported back to my bedroom, the bright shimmer from the full moon streaming in through my window. I yanked the curtains closed and took off pieces of clothing as I walked to the bathroom. Determined to rid myself of any physical reminder of the evening, I found a match in a drawer, lit it, and tossed it onto the clothes. Mesmerized by the bright orange glow, I wished the blaze would encompass me and the house. Flames flickered, the fire devouring the fabric. Heat and pulsing light danced toward me, but the tendrils extinguished at my feet, as if running into a block of ice.

Naked and void of feeling, I leaned over the tub and secured the drain before filling the basin with hot water, not even touching the cold water handle. Steam rose, and I slipped into the tub. Although my skin turned red, I could feel nothing, and I hoped the burning liquid would strip at least one layer of flesh, ripping away some part of me.

My body barely registered any heat, but my muscles started to loosen, and I found a small bit of reprieve, which only heightened my guilt and torment. Somewhere, Cecily gloated, awash in her triumph, or so I imagined. Her face had registered nothing but victory and happiness as she watched her sister and the boy Cecily professed to love dragged into the bowels of Hell.

What kind of person shows absolutely no remorse?

Me. Once. The weight of my answer hit me in the gut, and I sat up, water sloshing over the side of the tub, as I struggled to breathe. Memories of the night Dominick died were seared into my mind, and they flashed before me. In the moment his neck cracked, I'd felt brief moments of sorrow and regret. But with each passing day after, pain and justification fueled me.

Unaware how long I sat there, overcome with memories and emotions, I became lucid when I registered my teeth chattering and pulled the plug with my toe, not moving until the last bit of water drained away. I stood, catching a glimpse of myself in the mirror. A few marks showed from the demon's claws, though I knew they'd be gone by morning. If only my heart could heal as fast as my body.

Grabbing my robe and slipping it on, I trudged over to my bed, sitting on the edge, staring ahead but not registering anything before me. All I could see was the demon, the sulfurous smell that emanated from him overtaking my olfactory senses. His hot breath still burned my skin, as if he were in the room with me. His deep laughter gained volume in my mind. I pressed my fingers into either side of my head as I curled into myself and fell back onto the bed, enveloping myself in covers.

※

"Natalia."

Someone kept repeating my name. I fought against it, not wanting to leave the comfort of sleep. It was if someone called to me through water, the sound of the voice so muffled.

Then, I saw the demon again, standing before me, waving me toward him. I turned away, determined to escape his clutches, but I struggled, as if swimming against a riptide. I'd been caught in one once while vacationing with my mom on the California coast. From ashore, she yelled for me to stop fighting and relax, but it seemed such a foreign concept. Then another voice—soft and far away, a whisper I barely registered—had entered my head, telling me to let go. Later, sitting on the beach wrapped in my mother's arms, I imagined an angel had spoken to me.

But there was no such thing as angels; at least, none concerned with my wellbeing, my life was evidence of that.

"Natalia."

No. Fight it, I yelled in my mind.

"Natalia, please."

A shimmer of light cut through the darkness of my mind. I recognized the voice. *Rebecca.* I pried one eye open and then the other, surprised at the amount of energy the simple act required.

"Oh, thank God," Rebecca said, her hand flying to her chest. "I thought you were lost to your own torment. Your rantings didn't make sense, and I couldn't wake you."

I tried to sit up, but I only managed to lift my head a little. Rebecca responded to my efforts by jumping off the bed and fluffing a few pillows up behind my neck.

"I wish I were dead. But death isn't a luxury afforded to me," I said.

"Don't talk like that." She sat back down on the bed beside me, resting her hand on my arm, which was still under the covers. "What happened? You look like you were hit by a truck last night."

"If only," I muttered.

"Maybe some coffee will help. I'll be right back."

She flitted out of the room before I could stop her. I considered telling her to go home, to stop worrying about me, but I knew she'd only hover more if I resisted. She reminded me of my mom that way. From time to time, I wondered what had happened to her and if she'd searched for me. But I never wanted her to see what her only child had become.

"Here you go." Rebecca came back into the room carrying a mug with steam billowing from it and a brown paper bag. "And I brought you an apple turnover. Your favorite."

"Just lay them beside the bed." I maneuvered myself into a seated position.

"So," she said, drawing out the word as she sat in the chair opposite me. "What happened last night?"

She was like a dog with a bone, and I knew she'd hang around until I assuaged her fears about my state of mind. In reality, she was a few years older than me, but nobody would ever know, my mental age was multiplied ten-fold by the horrific things I'd done. Then, a thought took over. Maybe, if she knew what a monster I was, she'd run far away and spare herself the burden of caring for me, of having such an evil touch her life.

"I sent an innocent young man and woman to Hell last night." I let the words fall between us, watching her reaction.

Not even a twinge of horror crossed her features, though she stood and began pacing the room. "I thought we talked about me helping you vet cases so you wouldn't have to do anything like that ever again."

Will she ever see me for the monster I am? "Did you not hear me? I sent an *innocent* young man and woman to Hell last night. They struggled and begged for mercy, but I did what I had to do anyway. Besides, the young lady who ordered it was here before you and I made our bargain."

"Connor and Abigail?"

I opened my mouth to respond, but shock kept words from coming. How could she know?

"When I arrived this morning, I heard you moaning and came up here right away. You kept saying their names and thrashed about as you screamed 'no' and 'please' repeatedly, tears streaming down your face."

Without thinking, I reached up and felt the moisture on my face.

"I could tell you were tormented by something," she said.

"Don't you dare feel sorry for me." I tossed the covers aside and threw my legs over the edge of the bed, stopping for a second as a wave of lightheadedness took over.

Rebecca was by my side in a flash. "Here, let me help."

I slapped her hand away. "No. When are you going to see that you'd be better off far, far away from me?"

"Never. And when are you going to stop trying to convince me to leave?"

"Never," I said.

"Then, I guess we're at an impasse. I say we start our new arrangement today." She then went on to detail how she'd become my personal assistant, taking over my office—a space I rarely used—to do research on the people who came requesting revenge. She'd be there to ask questions of the visitors, stalling them if she felt further research was required. During the slow times, she'd acquire new books for me and continue doing my shopping and making meals. She requested a small salary, a higher food and shopping budget, and for me to purchase a laptop for her.

I felt the beginning of a smile creep onto my face, and no matter how much I tried to counteract it, the damn thing grew.

"And I want to research possible solutions to your problem. You wouldn't believe what you can find on the internet these days. Maybe I can find a spell—"

My smile immediately turned into a scowl. "I'll pay you double what you ask, and you can meet with all the clients and gather their information before I'll consider their requests, but under *no* circumstances are you to play with magic."

"But—"

"No buts. It's a non-negotiable term of your employment. If I catch you looking into anything magic-related, I'll send you away. Do you understand?"

She nodded.

"You told me you don't know your father, about your witch ancestry. Maybe I could look into that."

As I opened my mouth to reiterate my conditions, I hesitated, pondering the possibilities. Knowing more about him, about my lineage, might have helped me before that fateful night long ago, but the knowledge couldn't change my curse, my fate.

"Thanks. I truly appreciate it, but it's too late."

Rebecca hopped up and started fussing about the room, opening the curtains and choosing some clothes for me, which she laid at the foot of the bed. "Let's get you up and moving. It's closer to lunch than breakfast, so I'll make a quiche and bake some bread."

As she scurried out of the room, I went through the motions of getting ready, knowing she'd come back to hurry along the process if I didn't move fast enough. My thoughts kept returning to my father, to how little I knew about him, and I couldn't think of him without thinking about my mother. I missed her, but I knew bringing her back into my life would've only created heartache for both of us. As much as I longed for her to envelop me in her arms and make everything better, I knew that could never be, and seeing the hurt in her eyes when she realized what I'd become would've been unbearable.

Something deep inside me compelled me to my closet and to the one thing I had of my father's. The spell book. I pulled it down from the top shelf and blew off the dust on the cover, coughing as the particles flew into my mouth and nose. I sat on the edge of my bed and opened the book. Strangely enough, I'd only looked through it half a dozen times over the years. Not only did touching it remind me of Dominick, and the spell that started it all, but also the restrictions on my magnificent power.

Frustrated, I laid the book on the bed and started toward the stairs, the smell of lunch beckoning. A soft rush of air and the sound of paper rustling drew my attention, and I jerked my head back toward the bed. There, the spell book lay open, and I crept closer, equal parts hesitant and curious. A blank page stared back at me, but as I focused in on it, I noticed a beautiful script forming, slowly, as if someone wanted the words to form a piece of art, as if they were being written at that very moment. I fell to my knees before the tome and began to read, each word appearing just as I said the one before.

My dearest daughter, please know that I am with you always. Seek, and you shall find. Open your heart and believe again. Renew your faith, no matter how dark the pathway is. I love you. Your father.

My eyes darted back to re-read it, but the script had disappeared. I slammed the book shut and hurled it across the room, knocking my lamp over. Desperate to unleash my pent-up energy, I pounded my fists on the bed, the feel of the satiny spread unsatisfying.

Rebecca raced into the room. "Natalia, what's wrong?"

I needed to get out of there, to clear my head, so I stood, only to find Rebecca picking up the fallen lamp and then reaching for the spell book.

"I'll clean this up, and then I'll be right down."

She looked between me and the spell book, her eyes wide and her mouth slightly open. "Is this *the* book?"

"It is."

"Maybe I could look through it for you, see if I can find any answers."

Before I could stop her, she picked it up and flipped through the pages. I half-expected her to go flying across the room, the book protecting itself against those without magic, but it didn't happen. Instead, she turned it toward me.

"How odd. A blank spell book," she said.

Blank? I saw words, diagrams, handwritten notes—a page overflowing with material. "That *is* odd. Here"—I took the book from her—"I'll put it away. The darn thing is quite fickle." I wondered if my mom had ever tried to open it, if she, too, had only seen blank pages. It would make sense that only those with power could see the words.

Rebecca shrugged. "Come on downstairs; your tea is ready, and lunch is almost done."

My stomach growled, and I chuckled. Life has a way of humbling a person. No matter how much power I had, how many times I'd pondered the meaning of life and how to undo my curse, I was still beholden to simple things like hunger.

For the following hour, Rebecca and I chatted about her mother's upcoming wedding while enjoying a lovely lunch. As she was clearing up the dishes, the doorbell rang. When I started toward the front of the house, Rebecca waved me off and went to greet the visitor. I hoped for the simplicity of a package delivery, but I soon heard the sound of a young male voice. Males rarely sought me out, and curiosity sent me into the front room.

"Natalia, this is Peter. Peter, Natalia is the woman you seek." Rebecca motioned for him to sit in a nearby chair while she and I took seats close to him.

"I was told by a friend you were the woman to... help me."

I couldn't help but notice how he wrung his hands as his eyes darted around the room.

"My mother begged me to come..."

Hearing him mention his mother sent tingling sensations up and down my spine, shivers racking my body. My throat tightened, and my chest felt heavy, like someone had dropped a boulder on top of me. I had to get out of there.

"Please, excuse me." I motioned toward Rebecca. "My assistant will take down all your information, and we'll be in contact shortly."

"But—"

I rushed out of the room before I could hear any more. It took everything I had not to force him out the front door, to save him from himself. *Maybe this new situation with Rebecca will lessen my torture.* For what felt like an eternity, I paced back and forth in the kitchen before Rebecca came back into the room. She looked shaken. Her skin had lost two shades of color, and her hands trembled as she handed me a piece of paper with his information.

"Are you okay?" I asked.

"He told me an evil witch killed his father and uncle and left his sister a vegetable. She sits in a room, rocking back and forth in an old wooden chair, saying repeatedly how she made a mistake. His mom isn't much better. He says she blames herself and won't leave his sister's side."

My insides clenched as I brought the piece of paper closer and read the name at the top. A last name that conjured up horrific images of a father paying the price for what his brother had done.

Chapter 7

"He refuses to leave. Says his mother begged him to come here and ask for vengeance on her, to pay her back for her catastrophic mistake. Do you know what he's talking about?"

I placed a hand on the kitchen table for support and sank into the chair, the weight of my soul crashing in on itself.

A father.

His brother.

Mistaken identity.

Vignettes of the scene pulse in my head, one image after another.

"Fate is toying with me yet again." I meant to say the words in my head, but they came pouring out.

"Tell me. I can't help you if I don't know everything."

Another cruel twist. Rebecca was the only person on the planet, besides my mother, that I wanted to protect from the details of my deeds. I cared about Rebecca, and I didn't want to lose her. *How many times can she look the other way because of the one right I'd managed in so many years? Even if that right* had *benefitted her.*

"I know I've explained to you before that I can't refuse a request, no matter what the circumstances. That boy"—I gestured toward the living room—"lost his father by my hand. *His innocent father.* Phoebe, his sister, had come seeking vengeance against the man who'd raped her for many years. She named her father as the assailant, but her mother showed up as I was killing him—in a very unkind way, my rage at the man's acts leaving me without remorse—with the twin brother. The real perpetuator."

Rebecca's hand flew up to cover her gasping breath, her face contorted in horror—her eyes huge saucers, and her forehead creased.

"I'll never forget the sister's reaction. All the color drained from her face, and she threw up multiple times, until she dry heaved, nothing more to give. The mother cradled the girl, but she kept crying while the mother apologized repeatedly. There was nothing I could do."

I said the last part as much for myself as for Rebecca, who laid her hand on my upper back.

"Of course not. What a horrible tragedy. We have to do something for him, for that family." Her voice dripped with the high pitch of desperation.

By assisting me, her heart was breaking. She didn't deserve to know about the underbelly of humanity. *What have I done by involving her?* My thoughts turned to the boy. It would unburden both me and Rebecca to do the right thing by him.

"I can't go in there. If I do, and he makes the request for his mother, another tragedy will occur. She doesn't deserve to die, although I'm sure she feels that she does." Then a thought exploded in my head, a possible way to lessen the boy's load and end my suffering.

"What if you can convince him to take out vengeance on the person who really deserves it?" I didn't mean to be cryptic with the question, but I was still processing my idea. "After all, I'm the witch who took his father from him. Who killed an innocent man."

Her face twisted into various wrinkles as she seemed to understand what I was asking of her.

"No. Absolutely not," she said, backing away from me. "I will *not* go in there and sentence you to death."

I stood and covered the distance between us in two giant steps, taking her hands in mine. "No, don't think of it that way. You'll be releasing me from this curse."

She pulled away, shaking her head. "What, so you can go to Hell? It'd be like condemning a cop to the prison where he'd sent a bunch of criminals. I couldn't live with myself. I can't. There has to be another way."

Before I could say another word, she bolted from the room. I wanted to follow her, to convince her, but I couldn't risk being in the room with the boy who held the power to condemn me to murdering his mother.

I strained to hear the voices in the living room to no avail. Feeling like a caged animal, I moved about the small space, busying myself with useless tasks, including reorganizing the junk drawer.

When the front door slammed, I jumped a foot into the air, the sound ricocheting through my body. I willed myself to move, but by the time I convinced my feet to do anything, Rebecca stood before me, tears streaming down her face.

"That poor guy. It was all I could do to convince him to leave. I told him what you told me about that night's events. About how you can't undo a request—"

A sense of foreboding wrapped itself around my mid-section, causing uncomfortable cramps to ransack my abdomen. "You can't tell people about my curse. At least, I don't think we can. I can't put others' lives in danger by knowing too much about me."

"Anyway, I asked him if he wanted his mom's murder on his hands, and he said no, told me I was quite wise, saying he knew the pain his mother and sister went through daily after his father's death."

My body went numb. "You know that might have been my only hope."

"Going to Hell isn't hope. And Peter would've still lived with the regret of killing someone who didn't deserve it. You don't deserve it, especially for his father's death."

I ran a hand through my hair and blew out a long breath. "I can't ask you to do this. To be the go-between. I won't allow this curse to darken your heart like it has mine."

"I won't leave you. I've prayed long and hard about this, and I know God wants me in your life. Wants me to help you. He still loves you. I know that, and I love you, too."

If my heart still had the capacity for love, I would've said the sweet words back to her. But I couldn't. Love was a dirty four-letter word in my world. And although I knew her faith was strong, mine had suffered one too many blows.

"If there's a God, he would've struck me down long ago."

"When was the last time you read the Bible? I know you have one in the drawer by your bed. When's the last time you opened it?"

Every time I considered reading it, I stopped, knowing I'd only find hope there. And hope had become my greatest pain.

"Colossians 1, thirteen and fourteen, states: For He has rescued us from the dominion of darkness and brought us into the kingdom of the Son He loves, in who we have redemption, the forgiveness of sins." She whispered the words, her head bent.

An argument brewed in me, but fighting her would only bring more verses. I couldn't afford for one of them to puncture my tough exterior. I couldn't enter the fairytale land of angels and salvation any more or slide down the rabbit hole of lost hope.

"I appreciate your words. And I bet you have more verses you could quote me about forgiveness and God's love. Am I right?"

She nodded, her lips stretching into a huge smile. "Many more. It's kind of the crux of the Bible, you know?"

If I never did another good thing in my life, I could endure the fires of Hell knowing I did right by Rebecca. "Point taken. Could I bother you with a huge favor?"

Her eyes lit up. I so rarely asked her for anything. "Of course."

"I've been craving pecan pie. Haven't had it in—"

"Oh, my mom makes the best pecan pie. She roasts the pecans first. It's to die for."

Ah, the irony. But I needed a few hours alone, and having a slice of pie later was a great bonus. "Do you think she'd make me one? A little something sweet would really turn this day around."

Playing on her desire to always make things better, I fluttered my eyelashes and tilted my head toward her. "Please."

"Consider it done." She grabbed her purse from the kitchen counter. "I'll be back with a pie by dinner, and I'll make you some fried chicken and mashed potatoes tonight."

"Thanks. I truly appreciate it." I escorted her to the front door and waved as she left. I clicked it closed and leaned against it once I was alone, grateful for the silence.

Craving a distraction from the prior few days' events, too spent to pore over them anymore, I went to my office and pulled out an adult coloring book—a gift from Rebecca the previous Christmas—and some markers. I flipped through the pages. Flower-filled scenes ran to the edges of the paper, and I pushed them away. I didn't deserve beauty. Of any kind.

Sitting there, staring into space, a vision of Selene appeared, and along with it, her words about how to end the curse. *You can only end the curse by taking the life of someone you love.* Yet, even in that, I'd be doomed.

Lost in my thoughts, I barely registered the chime of the doorbell. I glanced at my watch. Too early for Rebecca. I sighed and didn't even bother to hope for a package delivery. With heavy footsteps, as if I trudged through just-poured cement, I made my way to the door.

A woman's back was to me. She turned slowly, my heart pounding with an odd sense of familiarity. When she faced me, I gasped.

"Mom?"

Chapter 8

"Natalia?"

As soon as the last syllable of my name left my mother's mouth, she launched herself at me, wrapping her arms around me and squeezing, nearly knocking me to the ground. After I steadied myself, I breathed for a few seconds and then gave in to the embrace.

Mom's body convulsed with sobs, and I could feel her wet tears falling onto my shoulder. Emotions swirled through me, feelings I hadn't experienced in a long time, but then questions arose, taking over and forcing my brain to come out of the emotion-induced fog.

I pulled away enough to guide her to the couch, sitting down next to her.

"I don't even know where to begin," I said. More than that, I couldn't decide which question to ask first. As I considered my options, she spoke.

"I'm confused. I wished for something, which led me to your door. *Your* door. After all these years, and all the prayers and desperate pleas to God to help me find you, and in my darkest moment, the split second I do something drastic and desperate, you appear. I just don't understand."

Internal warning signals sounded as I took in her words and began to realize what they meant. There was only one way to find me. Only one wish or heart's desire brought someone to my door.

Vengeance.

No, no, no. Not Mom.

I fought to keep my breathing steady and not panic, but I never was able to hide much from my mother.

"Sweetie, are you okay?" she asked.

Years disappeared, as if we hadn't lost any time together. She knew me like no one else, but that would only make everything more difficult. I needed to get her back out of my life before she figured out the monster her daughter had become, or worse… something horrible happened that I couldn't stop.

"Mom. Please, know that I love you, but you have to leave. So much has changed." As hard as I tried, I couldn't stop my voice from shaking. "I'm not your little girl anymore. Haven't been since…" I choke on the words, unable to force them out.

"Dominick. They came to the house looking for you when they found his body. His mother came out of the woodwork to say you'd murdered him."

Rage, an emotion I knew all too well, exploded in my brain, elevating my body temperature and sending shooting pains between my temples.

"That bitch!"

"Natalia, language." Mom lowered her voice and shook her head. "I raised you better than that."

Anger turned to manic humor, and I couldn't stop the cackle that exploded from my mouth.

"Honey, you're scaring me."

Oh, the continued irony, I thought. She had no clue just how terrifying I could be. I wanted to tell her all my misdeeds, send her away. Keep her safe. But another one of my endearing qualities kept me from doing that. Selfishness. I'd missed my mother. Maybe just a few hours with her would heal something in my soul and give me a few moments of happiness.

"I'm sorry. I didn't mean to. But I won't lie to you. I've changed, and not into something you can be proud of, but I *have* missed you. More than I can explain. Can you give me the rest of today?"

Mom answered before I could continue. "I'll give you more than that. My heart broke the day you left. And, so you know"—she took my hand—"I never believed you'd hurt Dominick. I know how much you loved him."

I flinched, as if a dagger had been thrust into my chest and caused the piercing pain in my heart. Unable to look her in the eyes, I lowered my head and concentrated on the fabric of my pants. "Mom, there are some things you don't—"

She placed a finger on my lips. "Shh. Right now, none of that matters. What does matter is that I came here, and I found my daughter. And I can feel joy in my heart again."

Came here. The words echoed in my head, reminding me of the dangerous game I was playing. She sought vengeance.

"Mom, let's make a deal. We'll have this day, more than I ever thought I'd have with you again, but then I must send you away. Before I do, I'll tell you everything. And I only ask one thing in return."

She scooted closer and took my hands in hers. "Anything."

"Don't ask just yet how I know this, but I know you came for revenge. If you ask it of me, I'll have no choice but to grant it." As soon as the last word fell from my lips, a blinding pain imperiled my ability to speak and breathe. I struggled, falling back against the couch cushions, darkness working its way from the edge of my vision and threatening to take over. *Guess that answers my question about whether I can share too much about my curse.* I had to tread lightly. If anything happened to my mother, I'd never forgive myself.

Mom disappeared for a bit as I gasped for air. When she returned, she had a cool rag and some water. She wiped my brow and hummed, something she always did whenever I was sick as a little girl. And it took me back to a time before the curse, when faith and love permeated every thought, when I'd known nothing of the cruelty of the world.

"Baby, there's nothing you could tell me that would make me love you any less. I'm your mother. Nothing can change that."

Hope flitted into my heart again, and I allowed it. No matter how much worse it made life going forward, I needed to believe again in that moment.

"Do you remember your favorite thing to do when you were little?"

I had to toil through the grisly memories at the forefront of my mind and access the images from my youth, the ones pushed back into the recesses of my brain. For much of my life, it had only been me and Mom. We'd loved to bake, spending hours in the kitchen coming up with our own spin on recipes we found in books. Some concoctions were complete failures, but we'd laugh and try again. Our pastor put us in charge of the church bake sales year after year because we brought in so much money.

With one eyebrow lifted and an expectant look on her face, Mom stared at me. I realized I'd been in my own head and hadn't answered her question. "Baking." As more memories surfaced, I chuckled. "What about that time we made a pecan pie with bacon?"

She threw her head back and laughed. "It sounded like such a brilliant idea at the time, but..." A shiver took over her body, and she scrunched up her face and pursed her lips. "That was just gross."

We reminisced about our other successes and failures. Then, without warning, a frown formed on my mother's face, and she turned from me. "When you disappeared, there were so many rumors."

"Mom, please, don't—"

"Rumors about witchcraft and you being your father's daughter. He broke my heart when he left, but I never hated him. Not until you disappeared. I blame him and that damned spell book. That night you ran out—" A sob choked off her words, and I placed my hand on her back. "I looked in your room for some sign of what was wrong. When I noticed that book missing, I knew you were dabbling in something you didn't understand. Couldn't understand because your father left you with a dangerous tool but no information.

"From that day, I wanted him dead. Wanted him to suffer like I suffered…"

Thunder clapped overhead, as if something wanted to warn me to stop her. "I've spent a lot of time on blame, and I can promise you it doesn't solve anything. We're all responsible for our own actions. A horrible thing happened to me.

I wrongly blamed Dominick and wished for his death…"

I took a breath. I should have known Fate wouldn't even give me a few hours of happiness with my mother.

"Yes, the spell book led me to the woman who could carry that death out." I started to say Selene's name, to show Mom just how twisted the tale truly was, but I feared an onslaught of pain. But more than anything, I wanted to finally take responsibility out loud and to someone I truly loved.

Love. A horrifying thought filled my head. *You can only end the curse by taking the life of someone you love.* Terror ran up my spine, causing me to stiffen. Then, an all too familiar sensation brushed against my skin, causing the flesh to prickle.

"Well, look at the amazing opportunity that's presented itself."

I cringed at the sound of Selene's voice and looked up to see the horror on my mother's face, her mouth gaped open and her eyes glossed over.

"What is that awful woman doing here?" She finally managed.

"Ah, so your daughter hasn't told you her story. Tsk. Tsk. Do tell, Natalia."

"What are you doing here, Selene?" I bent my head, defeat and despair flooding me, and turned to face her, cringing before I allowed myself to meet her gaze.

"As if you don't know. You asked to be released from your curse, and I told you the way. And here, before you, is someone I know you love. I figured you'd want me here."

I stood, pushing back my shoulders and commanding as much space as I could. I couldn't show her a moment of weakness or allow her to see any emotion. She'd destroyed me too many times. "I'd rather burn in Hell."

"That's a given. But now, or later, after many more people die by your hand? Innocent lives lost to your bloodlust."

Hatred filled me, and I took a step toward the evil woman. But when I tried to continue forward, she made a motion with her hand. Cold permeated my body. I couldn't move.

"You can't touch me, silly girl." She snickered.

From the corner of my eye, I saw my mom bolt forward. "Don't you dare—"

Another hand movement from Selene, and my mom stood transfixed about a foot away from me.

Selene moved closer to me and locked her gaze with mine. "You don't want to take her life?"

I tried to shake my head or form a word, to no avail.

"Silly me, I forgot." She touched her finger to the tip of my nose, allowing feeling to return to my head and face.

"No. Let her go."

She shook her head and spun to face my mother. "Seems you aren't here for the purpose I thought. But, wait, don't you have a wish? Something you came here to ask for?"

I opened my mouth to scream for my mother not to say another word, but Selene silenced me with a slight flick of her finger in my direction. My mouth clamped shut.

My mother grunted, and Selene must have realized she'd left Mom paralyzed, because the witch made a hand gesture, allowing Mom to inhale deeply.

"Now, you *must* request the wish of your daughter."

Bile filled my throat, and I swallowed it down, falling to the ground as Selene's magic faded away and mine surged. I scrambled over to my mom, but my heart sank. I was too late.

As if in a trance, her eyes staring off into the distance, and her face so still it seemed to be sculpted in stone, she said, "I wish for you to find your father and cause him the pain and suffering he's caused me."

Chapter 9

"Enough!" I yelled. Although I thought my heart had long ago blackened to the point of atrophy, it still shattered. Nothing could stop what was about to happen, but I refused to let my mom say another word, to add anything to the request. I directed my anger at Selene. "You've accomplished what you came here to do, and you know I'm at the mercy of her request, so leave."

"As you wish." She disappeared, her eerie cackle left behind in a muted tone. But the sound never left me.

With Selene gone, Mom came to and collapsed on the couch. "What just happened? What have I done?"

"We don't have much time." I could feel the edges of my vision collapsing, and before I could say another word, we transported to an area deep in the forest. As many times as I'd come into the woods to fulfill people's wishes, I never knew exactly where we were. I assumed it was some dark spot in Hell where all atrocities happened.

Mom appeared beside me, swaying, and I reached out and grabbed her.

"Where are we? I don't understand. Please tell me what's happening." Her words rang of desperation, the pitch changing almost by the syllable.

"Thanks to my own desire to exact revenge on Dominick, I was cursed to forever perform spells of vengeance. Once commanded to do so, I can't change the request, and it can't be rescinded."

She shook her head and then reached up with her hands to steady the motion. "No. I just… no. Oh my God. What have I done? I had one low moment, one shaking of my fist at Heaven and demanding your father feel what I'd felt. To know my pain. But I didn't…"

I took her hand. "I know. Too often, we say something in the heat of the moment, without thinking, and we don't realize the devastation it can cause. My punishment for my own misjudgment was this curse. And I've paid many times over for what I did to Dominick. Yet, it still doesn't seem like enough. He's dead because of me."

A flash of light filled the space, and I threw my palm up to shield my eyes until the brightness dimmed enough for me to let my hand drop. Astounded by the vision before me, I blinked, trying to see more clearly. But nothing changed. A man clothed in white fabric lowered to the ground, his wings pulling in to rest at his sides. His bare feet seemed to float over the ground as he moved toward me.

"My dear Natalia." He reached out and touched my face, and I sank into the warmth for a second.

"Daniel. Is that you?"

My mother's voice brought me back from the euphoria I lost myself to, and I refocused, opening my eyes.

"Yes. I've missed you, my love. Both of you."

As if time stood still, none of us moved. Then, Mom, in a voice barely above a whisper, asked, "Why did you leave us?" Tears glistened on her cheeks, and a new one slipped from the corner of her eye.

Dad caught it with the top of his finger. "So many forces lined up against our family. I left to protect you, to try and find the coven who wanted us all dead." He turned to me. "You were so young, the sweetest thing I'd ever seen. I couldn't let them hurt you. But I left the spell book behind and put a protection spell on you and your mother."

"But they found us anyway," Mom said.

"The more Natalia used the book, the easier she was to find. As magic began to cling to her, forces could sense it."

Overburdened by the weight of responsibility, I fell to my knees and leaned forward, placing my forehead on the ground. I'd led Selene to us, and I'd fallen for her trap, condemning me to an eternity of pain and suffering, and ruining my mother's life in the process.

Warmth and light encompassed me as my tears began to fall.

"My child, I never left you. Even during your darkest moments, I was with you. Standing by your side. Loving you."

All my emotions rushed forward, and the dam ruptured. I cried like I never had before, tears flowing and sobs racking my body. Despair wrapped its talons around me. To know my father had witnessed every horrific thing I'd ever done broke me. I was no stranger to shame, but I experienced it on a whole new level.

"Natalia, look at me," my father said.

Every part of my body felt heavy, as if the burden of my life pinned me to the ground. I struggled to lift my head, my eyes still blurred with tears. Finally, my eyes connected with his.

"You have so much more strength than you think. You can end this."

At some point, Mom had joined me on the ground and wrapped her arms around me. We sat in our cocoon for several minutes.

"What do I do?" Four simple words emptied my soul.

My parents stood, and my dad offered me a hand. I placed one foot on the ground and then the other, testing the strength in my legs. Although I wobbled, I managed to rise.

"You have to figure that out for yourself. And I know you can. It's been within you the whole time, but you have to forgive yourself. Forgiveness on the other side awaits… you only have to ask."

Tears threatened again, and I swallowed down the lump in my throat.

"And you won't have to do it alone. I'll be there for you, too," Mom said as she draped her arm over my shoulders.

"Well, well, well. What a touching family moment."

I jerked my head toward the unmistakable malevolent voice. Selene. In one second, I went from a childlike hope of salvation to having murderous thoughts.

"Daniel," she said. Her footsteps toward him seemed calculated and menacing; she took her time, matching her pace to the rhythm of her words. "It seems only yesterday that I ordered your death, taking my own vengeance, of course. Revenge for all the power your family stole from mine."

Fed up with her constant meddling in my life, I took a step to confront her, but my father straightened his arm in front of me and shook his head.

"Natalia, my dear, you have no choice but to carry out your mother's wishes." Selene's voice was bordering on a hiss.

"It's been done," my father said, his voice booming in the small clearing. "Her mother asked that I suffer as she has suffered. And I have. I suffer each day watching my daughter crumble underneath a curse you placed on her. And worse, I've watched lately as she agonizes over every decision and action."

Selene opened her mouth slightly but then slammed it shut again. Blood dripped from her hands, pinned against her sides, as her nails dug deeply into the flesh.

I inhaled, ready to calmly dismiss the hag, but my mother spoke first. "So, as you can see, you aren't needed here."

"As I see it, you're the one who's not needed here." In a flash, Selene threw her hands together and formed a ball of fire, hurling it at my mother.

Gut instinct took over, and I flung my body in the pathway, both palms in front of me to deflect the blow. It sailed to the side, but Selene kept coming, throwing more and more. I blocked some with my body—my curse both a power and a shield—and my father formed a force field of light around our family.

Then, a wail, like many I'd heard as a result of the pain I'd inflicted, sounded behind me, and I spun to see the demon from before behind my mother, his claws protruding through her chest. Blood seeped through the front of her shirt as her knees buckled.

The demon glared at me. "Ah, my lovely, we meet again. Are you coming home soon?"

"No!" I willed my power toward the beast, pushing through the pain building in my skull. When I saw the explosion of light, I thought the miserable ache had finally consumed me. But as my vision cleared, I saw my mother in my father's arms. Selene and the demon had disappeared.

I crawled over to Mom. *No, no, no. Please, don't let her be gone.*

Her chest rose up and down in exaggerated movements, and her lips moved, a soft sound escaping. I leaned in closer to hear.

"I love you." Cough. "You're more than this curse." Heavy breathing. "Break it. You know how."

And with that word, a small hiss came out of her mouth, and her chest stopped moving, her head falling to the side. I collapsed on top of her, crying and begging her to come back.

"She is gone, my child," my father said.

Another death at my hands. She would've been safe if she'd never found me. Everything I touched suffered. I lost myself in blame and self-pity.

"This is evil's doing, not yours." My father lifted my chin to meet his gaze. Beside him, a small light flickered and grew. Slowly, the shape became defined, and I recognized the face.

Mother.

"Now, there are two of us looking out for you. Go, do what you must. You're stronger than you believe.

Chapter 10

"You've got to get out of bed." Rebecca turned on lights and scrambled about the room making noise. "It's been two days, and I can't watch you suffer anymore. You have to talk to me."

Desperation clung to her words, her voice high and cracking. I grabbed my pillow and placed it over my head. "Go away!" For two nights, I'd suffered through the nightmare of what happened to my mother, my mind going over and over it as I slept—the demon claws bursting through her chest a vision I couldn't shake.

"No!" She yanked the pillow off me. "Whatever has put you in this state, just tell me. Haven't I proven that I won't go anywhere? That I'm not leaving you."

"If you were smart, you'd go away and never return. I only hurt people." I sat up, and my brain cleared. During the sleeplessness over the previous forty-eight hours, a plan had begun to form in my mind. A plot to end things once and for all. And Rebecca played a very important part. I needed her.

"I'll be downstairs, making your breakfast. Please, come down." She turned, slumped, and walked out of the room.

Watching my mother die had been the last straw. I had to end things, but I would *not* take another life, especially the life of someone I loved. And the only person left that I loved—a fact that had become apparent during my tossing and turning—was downstairs making me breakfast. I wouldn't let anything happen to her. With a renewed spirit, I hopped out of bed, got dressed, and hurried downstairs.

When I walked into the kitchen, Rebecca's face lit up, and she brought me a steaming mug of coffee along with a croissant and some bacon. "I'm so glad you came down."

I sat at the table and motioned for her to join me. "Come, sit. I have something I want to talk to you about."

She pulled back a chair and took a seat. I detailed everything since I last saw her: meeting my dad, how he was an angel, and losing my mother. Rebecca's eyes glistened with tears.

"I'm so sorry."

"I think you can understand that I can't do this anymore. I won't let another person suffer because of me. And the only solution I can come up with is to ask Peter to come back. To have him seek revenge on me by requesting my death."

Rebecca started shaking her head, her lips pressed together in a thin line.

"I know." I took her hands. "But it's the only way. I'm willing to pay for what I've done. I'm already in my own personal Hell. Please, know that I need to end this. I just—" My voice broke, and I took a few seconds to breathe and remember what I had to do. "This has to be done. And Peter is my only hope. Will you please do this for me?"

Water filling her eyes, she looked away, pinching her lips together and looking skyward. I gave her a moment, not wanting to push. As I opened my mouth to restate my plea, she faced me again.

"I'll do what you need me to do. I wish there was another way, but…" Her words hung in the air.

"There's not."

"Then, what's next? I don't know him, so how will I get him to come back?"

I stood and went to my desk, pulled out a file folder, and returned to the table, sliding the packet to Rebecca. "There's everything you need to know." Seeing her upturned eyebrow and the tilt of her head, I continued. "For months, I've been compiling information on every client I've ever wronged, just in case I ever had the opportunity to help them."

"Something like what you did for me?" she asked, her fingers trembling as she opened the file.

"Yes. So far, you've been the only one. So, anyway, I've been desperate to find a way to assist this family, but as it turns out, I need their help. It seems wrong, but in a way, their tragedy will count for something. It will end the life of the person who did it and end my power to do it to anyone else."

She flipped through the pages. "I'll contact him. But what will happen to the curse?"

"Once I'm gone, it'll die with me. Although I don't put it past Selene to try and stop us. Let's just do this quickly, before she can get involved." I wished I had a better answer.

"Okay, I'll be back as soon as I have news." She gathered her things, including the folder, and hurried out the door.

Helpless, I fell to my knees and did something I hadn't done in a long time, something I'd started to believe in again. I prayed.

◦•✦•◦

Trying to quell my nervous energy, I'd paced about the house, tidying up and even reorganizing some library shelves. Every moment that passed increased my anxiety levels and the fear that Selene would visit.

When the front door blew open, slamming into the nearby wall, I jumped back, catching my foot on a pile of books and falling to the ground.

"Natalia, are you here?" I heard Rebecca call.

"Yes, coming." I scurried to my feet and raced down the stairs. Still slightly breathless, I extended my hand to the young handsome man before me. "Peter, thanks for coming."

He shook my hand. "Rebecca explained some of the situation, and… Well, she can be pretty convincing."

"How about we talk in here?" I gestured toward the living room. When Peter walked ahead,

I mouthed the words thank you to Rebecca, who nodded.

"I understand you want me to seek revenge on you for what happened to my father and for the pain and suffering my mother and sister have endured."

Hearing him say the words only further bolstered my commitment to convincing him to take my life. "Not just revenge. You must be very specific. I should die."

He looked from me to Rebecca, who cast her eyes downward, her hands clamped together so hard in her lap that her fingers were red.

"Only God should determine who lives and dies."

I wanted to fall to my knees and beg him to get on with it, to just utter the words to take my life. But I understood his statement all too well. "I agree. It took me way too long to figure that out for myself. And then I wished for Him to strike me down for thinking I had the right to determine who deserved punishment. I've done so many things wrong. My death will put an end to that."

"My sister thought killing my father, the man she thought raped her daily, was the answer. I can assure you, it wasn't. Her suffering has only multiplied."

Memories flooded into my mind, the horrified look on his sister's face when the uncle appeared. My throat stung and tears threatened. "If I could change that moment, if I'd known, I would've tried to talk her out of it. Like I did with Rebecca. But I didn't. And I saw a young girl in front of me who'd suffered so badly, so much like I had…" I swallowed. "I wanted to help her. I was wrong. I don't want to ever hurt anyone again."

"I forgive you."

His words cut like a knife.

"No, no, I'm not asking for forgiveness." I sat straighter, more determined than ever to convince him of what had to be done. "I need you to help me undo this horrible thing that I've become. I won't kill someone I love"—I cast a glance at Rebecca, hoping he'd understand—"to end this curse and be free. I don't deserve that. But I'll gladly accept my death and the punishment I face in Hell."

"And what of Selene?" he asked.

Confused and shocked, I turned to Rebecca.

"I told him everything. All the way back. He deserved to know. You're asking him to sentence you to death. He deserved to know." Her lips trembled as she spoke, and she avoided looking me directly in the eye.

"Selene will have to account for what she's done. If I could stop her, I would. But she'll no longer wield me as an instrument of destruction if you kill me." Desperate, I fell to my knees before Peter, taking his hands in mine. "Please, help me stop this."

He moved to the edge of his seat, slowly standing and pulling me up with him. "Natalia, I seek revenge on the woman who's brought about the destruction of so many. My clear wish is for you to kill Selene."

With his first words, my heart had soared, and I'd closed my eyes, eager to hear the request for my own life. But then I heard him say Selene, and my eyes darted open.

"Selene?"

But the question died on my lips as a sudden gust of wind blew my hair into my face and slammed me into Peter. As I struggled to regain my balance, Selene's voice echoed throughout the space.

"What trickery are you up to, you fool?" she shouted.

Power surged through me, and I realized Peter's wish had been granted. "I take no pleasure in this, although I should. You took advantage of a young girl, of her hurt, and you've wielded it to put a blight on this world. I promise you, I'll spend my days trying to make up for it and fighting this curse. No amount of pain will ever make me kill again in the name of revenge."

I took steps toward her, and she backed away. "Now, dear, you know the curse won't end. Not until you kill someone you love."

"I'll spend every waking moment praying for guidance. You have no power over me anymore, and I don't believe a word that comes out of your mouth. That ever did. You will no longer have power over me."

With her continued retreat, she backed into the far wall, and I covered the distance between us.

"I should make you endure some of the awful things my victims have, or at the very least, what the demons did to me. But I won't. I'm better than that. I'll end your life swiftly."

She opened her mouth, but I didn't hesitate. Not wanting to hear anything else she had to say, I unleashed every bit of power I had into her, my hands thrusting yellow light into her body and lifting her off the ground. I snapped her neck. Clean and quick, like she'd done to Dominick. Then, I collapsed—my power and emotions spent.

As I lay there, consumed with visions, someone's arms helped me up. My eyes cleared, and I could see Rebecca before me.

"Where's Peter?" I tried to make sense of it all.

"He said a few words and then disappeared. Just… he was just gone," Rebecca stuttered.

"What did he say?" I managed.

"He said, 'Tell her she must forgive herself, for only then will she truly be free.'"

Chapter 11

Two Months Later

"Natalia, are you here?" Rebecca yelled as she walked in the front door.

I greeted her, having just returned from the store.

"What have you been up to today?"

"Just a visit to the store and a walk through town. It's a beautiful day."

Ever since the day Selene's reign of tyranny ended, I'd been able to leave the house, and I hadn't had one visitor requesting revenge. Rebecca insisted the curse had been lifted, but I stayed guarded, not willing to fully embrace that hope. Maybe I'd been granted only a short reprieve. Death still awaited me, as it did us all. Even so, I was grateful, and I'd thanked God for it every day.

"I was also in town, and I ran into someone. Someone I'm sure you'll want to see."

Shivers ran up my spine, and I braced myself. As goosebumps rose on my arms, I swallowed down the fear building in my throat as Rebecca waved someone into the house.

"Hi," she said, her petite features even more frail than the picture in my mind. "Do you remember me?"

"I'll never forget. Please, come in, Phoebe," I said.

She sat on the couch, and I remembered the first time she'd been in my home, when she'd come seeking revenge against her father. I mulled over what to say to her, but she spoke first.

"I wanted to come here, to tell you that I was doing better."

Relief coursed through me, overtaking the fear that she'd visited for other reasons. "When your brother visited a couple of months ago—"

"My brother?" she asked, moving to the edge of her seat.

"Yes, he came to visit. He told us you were basically in a coma—"

"My brother's been dead for five years."

I couldn't contain my gasp, and I heard Rebecca's chime in with mine.

"But…" I didn't know what else to say.

She stood and paced in the small area in front of me, containing her steps to the nine-by-twelve Oriental rug in front of the couch. "It's all starting to make some sense to me. You see, he came to me while I was in my coma. Told me I had to forgive myself in order to heal."

Forgiveness—the same instruction he'd given Rebecca before he disappeared.

"I did. I forgave myself, and then I forgave my mother and worked with her so she could forgive herself. Now, I'm here to forgive you."

Still reeling, I tried to clarify some details. "So, your bother passed away five years ago." I sucked in a breath, realizing he'd died about the same time as Dominick. After shaking off the thought, I continued, "Yet he sat in this very house two months ago, and even once before then. Right, Rebecca? You were here."

She nodded.

Phoebe stopped dead in her tracks and turned to me, a huge smile overtaking her face. "That brother of mine, he sure has been busy as an angel."

Words eluded me, but Rebecca found hers and told the tale about our encounters with Peter. When she finished, Phoebe took my hand.

"It seems my brother has given you the time you need to forgive yourself. I hope you'll find it in your heart. For then, you'll be free, as I am now free." She kissed me on the cheek. "If you ever need anything, I hope you'll call on me or my mother."

I shook my head, still struggling to speak. In an intense state of confusion, I escorted Phoebe to the door and thanked her for coming.

Rebecca followed the young woman out.

Left alone, my thoughts bounced around, leaving me questioning everything. Determined to see what had changed, I ran upstairs and grabbed my father's spell book, searching for a simple tester spell. Light. I conjured light from the palm of my hand. It worked. Then, I tried another spell, my heart pounding.

Ever since Selene died, I feared another person walking through the door requesting revenge. No matter how much I swore I'd never again believe Selene's threats, I hadn't believed I'd been truly released from my curse.

As I floated a few books around the room, Rebecca came in. "What are you doing?"

"Magic, I'm performing magic. Regular magic."

~~~

That night, as I curled into my comforter and prepared for sleep, I knew I'd face the next morning with hope and a determination to seek out forgiveness. As I drifted off to sleep, I saw the faces of my mother, my father, and Dominick floating above me, their smiles filling my heart.

No one could know what tomorrow would bring, but I finally had something back, something that had been ripped from me.

Hope.

About the Author

Tia Silverthorne Bach has been married to her college sweetheart for twenty years, has three beautiful girls, and adores living in the breathtaking state of Colorado. Her daughters were born in Chicago, San Diego, and Baltimore; and she feels fortunate to have called many places home. She believes in fairy tales and happy endings and is an avid reader and rabid grammar hound.

She is an award-winning, multi-genre author and an Editor for Indie Books Gone Wild. From an early age, she escaped into books and believes they can be the source of healing and strength. If she's not writing, you can find her on the tennis court, at the movies, reading a good book, or spooning Jif peanut butter right out of the jar.

Connect with Tia online!
Blog: depressioncookies.blogspot.com
FB: www.facebook.com/tia.bach.author
Twitter: @Tia_Bach_Author
Goodreads: http://www.goodreads.com/author/show/4456703.Tia_Silverthorne_Bach

Other books by Tia Bach:

Heart Chatter - Depression Cookies I

2011 Readers Favorite Book Awards, Silver Realistic Fiction and Finalist Chick Lit
2011 Next Generation Indie Book Awards, Finalist Chick Lit

Two distinct voices, two stories interwoven within the walls of family and love.

Abby needs some magic in her life, along with a white knight, respectful children, and an exciting career plan. Instead she is drowning in unfulfilled expectations, disappointments, and unmet needs. What she doesn't expect is to find the true essence of magic in the strength, friendship, power, and energy of the female spirit found in her mother and her mother's zany group of friends. Krista cannot believe it's happening again. Her father waltzes in and announces another move. And what does her mother do? Nothing. Don't they realize she's almost thirteen, and this could mean the end of her life? In the midst of teenage melodrama, she is determined to survive a new school, defeat the annoyances of two scene-stealing sisters, and deal with out-of-touch parents. Yet she quickly realizes the double-edged sword of growing up.

Tala Prophecy Series

Chasing Memories
Chasing Shadows
Chasing Forgiveness
Chasing Destiny
Chasing Eternity

Fractured Glass: A Novel Anthology
7: The Seven Deadly Sins
Enchanted Souls
War and Pieces ~ Frayed Fairy Tales

Find them all on Amazon!

Made in the USA
Middletown, DE
25 March 2018